Don't Tease Me

A Dark Mafia Age-Gap Romance

Made Men

Renee Rose

Copyright © September 2022 Don't Tease Me by Renee Rose and Renee Rose Romance

All rights reserved. This copy is intended for the original purchaser of this book ONLY. No part of this book may be reproduced, scanned, or distributed in any printed or electronic form without prior written permission from the authors. Please do not participate in or encourage piracy of copyrighted materials in violation of the authors' rights. Purchase only authorized editions.

Published in the United States of America

Wilrose Dream Ventures LLC

This book is a work of fiction. While reference might be made to actual historical events or existing locations, the names, characters, places and incidents are either the product of the authors' imaginations or are used fictitiously, and any resemblance to actual persons, living or dead, business establishments, events, or locales is entirely coincidental.

This book contains descriptions of many BDSM and sexual practices, but this is a work of fiction and, as such, should not be used in any way as a guide. The author and publisher will not be responsible for any loss, harm, injury, or death resulting from use of the information contained within. In other words, don't try this at home, folks!

❧ Created with Vellum

Want FREE Renee Rose books?

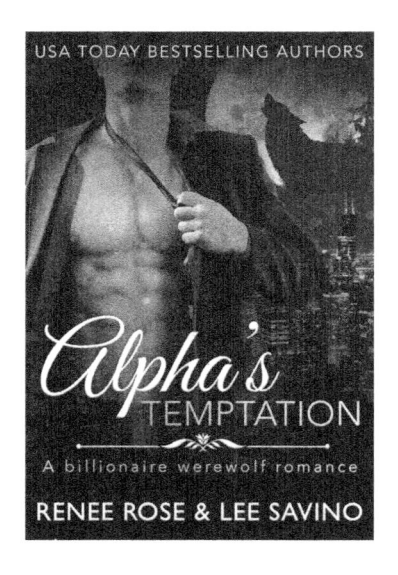

Go to http://subscribepage.com/alphastemp to sign up for Renee Rose's newsletter and receive a free copy of *Alpha's Temptation, Theirs to Protect, Owned by the Marine* and more. In addition to the free stories, you will also get bonus epilogues, special pricing, exclusive previews and news of new releases.

Don't Tease Me
Made Men Series Book 1

I own you now.
Desperate and alone, I strike a bargain with a mafia boss.

I make myself available to him. He pays my bills.

I'm his beck-and-call-girl. He's my sugar daddy.

Bobby Manghini owns me–that's our arrangement.

Giving myself to him is easy.

He may be older, but he's sinfully sexy. Skillful in bed.

It's a win-win for both of us, so long as I remember one thing:

Don't fall in love.

Bobby calls the shots, but he doesn't play for keeps.

I'm a toy, not his happily-ever-after.

The book is a lengthened and revised version of the previously published story Mob Mistress.

Chapter One

Lexi

L I land in Newark with nothing but coffee in my belly and an ache in my chest.

I should be thrilled. It was my first week of my new corporate job with a hair product company—a huge step up for an independent hair stylist.

I just observed a three-day workshop held for a packed hotel conference room in Vegas. As part of my training, I'll observe three more—in Denver, Los Angeles and Tucson, then take over as trainer, teaching them myself.

"Lexi Tyler?"

My head snaps up to find a grim-looking woman and blank-faced man dressed in suits blocking my way.

"Yes? What's going on?"

The woman flashes an ID card at me. "I'm Tracy McGalicaster from the FBI. We'd like to ask you some questions."

I try to peer around them, as if the answer lay in the carousel, with my suitcase. "Um…no, thanks," I fumble.

"It's not a choice," McGaliscaster says drily. "Sully will get your bag. Come with me."

I look around again, still somehow hoping someone might intervene, or explain they had the wrong person. The woman takes hold of my upper arm and begins to maneuver me through the airport and out to a waiting sedan.

Her companion arrives ten minutes later with my bag and climbs in beside me.

"What's going on?"

"We'll be asking the questions, Miss Tyler."

"About what?"

Neither agent answers.

I chew on my lip.

Bobby.

They want information on Bobby. This is what I get for getting involved with a mob boss. I should've known better. Not only has he bludgeoned my heart, but now my head's on the FBI's chopping block.

Cold dread washes through me.

They take me to a small office with nothing but a few chairs and a table. "Sit," the woman commands. Her chair scrapes the floor as she pulls it back, and the sound echoes against the blank walls.

I lick my dry lips, wishing I had a water bottle.

"Miss Tyler, you have been working as a hairstylist for how many years now?"

"Uh...twelve?"

"Are you asking me or answering me?"

I glare at the woman and say nothing.

She opens a file and shuffles some papers. "I have here your tax returns from the past twelve years. I have both state and federal. Never once, in all the twelve years did you claim any tips."

"So?" I grit my teeth.

"So, I find that unusual. Are you really that terrible at what you do that no one–in twelve years–ever paid you a tip?"

I fold my arms across my chest and glare.

"That seems unlikely. A better answer is that you have been defrauding the government, Lexi."

"That's ridiculous!" I sputter. "How much do you believe I make in tips a year? Not enough to pay taxes on them, I can tell you that. Did you happen to notice how much I earn a year? I'm not exactly in the highest tax bracket."

"It doesn't matter. You owe all your back taxes, plus interest and penalties. Then there are the legal ramifications. Tax fraud is tax fraud, and this case will be easy to prove."

I wait. I know there will be more.

"You're looking at jail time. And somehow I doubt your new employer is going to keep you on when they find out you have to take a leave of absence."

My fingernails dig into my arms where they tangled across my chest.

"Unless, of course, you choose to cooperate."

I say nothing. I've watched too many cop shows to not guess exactly where this conversation leads.

"We'd like information on Bobby Manghini," Sully says.

Chapter Two

Six Weeks Earlier

Bobby

I accept a Cuban cigar from my cousin Al and light it.

"You're late, *stronzo*," he busts my balls, even though the only thing I'm late for is a game of poker with the other Made Men. But it's his right to be the ball-buster. As the don of the Family, he's my boss and the guy I've looked up to my entire life.

"I know. Sorry. We had a shitshow at the office." We're in the private lounge at Swank, the nightclub built by my construction company as our outfit's unofficial headquarters.

"Anything I need to know about?" Al chomps on his cigar and swirls the ice in his highball glass.

"Nah." I shake my head. "Permit problems. The usual fuckery. Nothing I can't handle." I own and run the Family construction and real estate companies, which I keep mostly above-board, other than calling in favors and making deals with politicians. Joey launders the Family's dirty money through my business and the nightclub.

"You want me to handle someone, you just say the word." Carlo, our ruthless younger cousin from Sicily stacks his chips. He's Al's protege. Joey, Al's younger brother, is technically in line to inherit the throne, but I'm not sure his heart is in it the way Carlo's is. There may eventually be a showdown between the two for who becomes Al's right-hand man. For now, Joey is the mob's accountant. The only one of us who went to college.

"Glenlivit, on the rocks," I tell Gina, the cocktail waitress who comes in with a tray full of drinks for the men. She's banging Leo, one of the bouncers.

"Already got it for you, Mr. Manghini." She drops a cocktail napkin in front of me and sets the drink down.

"You take such good care of me, sweetheart." I hand her a hundred-dollar bill because I appreciate the fuck out of good service, and Gina works it.

She takes it but hesitates, and I look up. "Um, your... uh...*Stacy* is asking to see you."

Stacy. Fuck me. She was my last plaything. A stripper I set up in my downtown apartment to be available to me. It worked out for a couple of months, but she ended up being a pain in my ass. She has addictions–to cocaine, my money, and drama.

I cut her loose three weeks ago, but she misses her meal ticket.

"Could you handle *her* for me?" I ask Carlo, and the rest of the men at the table laugh.

He snorts. "I don't do sloppy seconds, *cugino*. Although she is hot. I might bang her once."

Carlo hasn't had a girlfriend since he moved to America. Like me, he seems to prefer strippers and no commitment. Although in his case, I suspect his hesitation to date has everything to do with Al's daughter, Summer. I've seen the way he watches her from across the room. The way he hovers protectively when she's near. I doubt he'll make a move on her, though, because Al would kill him.

"Tell her to get lost," I say.

It's not really fair of me to make Gina the messenger, but I'm done with this girl. Plus, I'm already sitting down, and Al's ready to start the game. I don't want to get up and deal with her myself. "If she won't go, have Leo throw her out."

"Got it." Gina's been moving swiftly around the room, emptying Al's ashtray and picking up used glasses.

"I'm sorry to make you the bad guy."

"No, it's cool." She pats the apron pocket where the $100 bill disappeared. "I've got your back with the ladies." Gina slips out the door.

Joey snorts as he deals the cards. "You having trouble handling your ladies, Bobby?"

"Yeah, fuck off, *stronzo*."

"No, but really." Al pins me with a tough-guy look. "Is this girl gonna be a problem?"

Aw, fuck. The Family gets real touchy about who we bring in and out of our lives. What they know. What happens to them when we cut them loose. Al's asking me if Stacy knows anything and is she crazy or manipulative enough to turn on me. To wear a wire and become an informant. Or to get in bed with one of the other organized crime families in the Tri-State area.

Basically, Al wants to know if Stacy actually needs to be dealt with. Because the Family does not like loose ends. Not even the ex-fucktoy variety.

"Nah, she's not a real problem. She's nothing," I say. I need to de-escalate this shit right away.

Joey takes a sip of his grappa. "Maybe if you stopped dating strippers and settled down with a real woman, you might not be getting stalked by your crazy exes."

"Where's *your* real woman?" I pick up my cards. "I don't see you bringing around anyone worth keeping."

"True, true," Joey admits. "But I'm looking. I also don't make a habit of keeping women on the side like you do."

"Yeah, what's up with that?" Al sets his cigar in the ashtray to fan his cards in front of his face. "It's like you still think you're married."

I divorced five years ago, and for the record, never kept a woman on the side while I had a wife, even when our marriage was shit. But Al's right, I'm definitely treating my women now as side pieces, not main events. That's the way I prefer it. I like to play sugar daddy.

"It's just easier." I shrug. "I take care of her financially, and she makes herself available to me. I'm the bossman. Works out great for both of us."

When I'm sugar daddy, there's an unspoken–or sometimes spoken–business arrangement. She receives financial benefit in exchange for being available to me. And I love holding power over my woman. It turns me on. I'm good to them–don't get me wrong. I spoil my girls rotten. And that's why I get to call the shots. If I want her on her knees, I tell her. If I want her over my knee, I put her there. I don't have to bring her to family events or introduce her to my daughters.

"Until she turns psycho." Carlo jerks his thumb toward the door leading to the main lounge.

"Yeah, there's that." I seem to let my dick do the thinking when it comes to women. Another reason to keep them in the periphery and not actually allow them into my life. In the business we're in, it's too dangerous. You can't mix psycho with *La Famiglia*. People will get killed. I'm definitely done with clingy crazy. My next arrangement is going to be clean. At the first sign of emotional attachment, I'm calling it off.

"What about you, Dean?" I change the focus of the conversation to one of the other soldiers whose wife gave birth six months ago. "How's family life?"

He chomps on his cigar. "Good, good. Olive is sitting up. Cute as fuck. Jessie's doing an amazing job with her."

"She's not pissed about you coming out with us tonight?"

He grins. "I negotiated a deal. I get to come to poker night, she gets a ladies' night, which is essentially just a book club where they drink wine and talk about dirty romance novels. She comes home all ready to put into practice what she's been reading, so it's a win-win for me."

We laugh. It sounds sweet, but no part of me misses having a woman to answer to.

I am never doing that shit again.

* * *

Lexi

I camp out on a barstool near the corner where the cocktail waitresses put their orders in and get their drinks made. I have no business being here considering every dollar I earned cutting hair this week needs to go to the rent on both my apartment and the salon, but it's Friday night, and I deserve a little fun. I need it. I'm at Swank, the nightclub where my best friend Gina works as a cocktail waitress.

"I just got a hundred-dollar tip." Gina appears at my

elbow and moves the glasses from her tray onto the bar. The bartender swiftly takes them and loads them into a dish rack below the bar.

"Are you serious? Damn, that's good money. They're not hiring now, right?"

The bartender, Stan, overhears and shakes his head as his hands fly mixing drinks.

"Do you think you could put in a word for me next time there's an opening here? I could use a few tips like that."

Gina hands Stan a ticket with her drink orders and flashes me a sympathetic look. She knows I'm in dire straits financially. A car accident this past year left me with a pile of medical bills, and for two months I couldn't work because I couldn't stand. I've been scrambling to catch up ever since without much luck. I'm currently three full months behind on rent at both my apartment and at the salon.

"You already work your ass off at the salon," Gina says. "You don't need a second job. What you need is a sugar daddy."

The guy standing near me–the one who has been moving closer and acting like he's going to strike up a conversation but hasn't worked up the nerve yet–gives a little scoff. I ignore him and roll my eyes at Gina. "I don't think that exists."

"Oh, it exists," she says with total conviction. She tips her head toward the back room, the private area where the owners hang out. I know who she means. Swank is owned by the mafia.

"Those guys?" There's no way I'm getting involved with that crazy stuff. "No thanks."

"You should just let me introduce you. There's one guy in particular who might be perfect for you."

"The heavy tipper?" I don't know why I'm even asking.

I am not interested in this idea of hers. Not at all.

"Yes–the heavy tipper. He's hot and plays sugar daddy."

I sense the guy beside me wanting to insert himself in the conversation again, but I continue to ignore him.

"You better be careful, if Leo hears you say another guy is hot, he'll tear the guy's head off." Leo is her heavily-tattooed and muscled boyfriend who works as a bouncer at Swank.

He's crazy about Gina but also possessive and jealous when it comes to her attention.

"Well, not this guy, but yeah. He'd want to." Her gaze automatically goes across the club to where Leo's standing by the door looking every inch the beefy badass bouncer. He catches her looking, and they share a smile. Her expression momentarily goes mooney. It's very cute. I have to admit sometimes I'm jealous of what they have.

The bartender finishes making all Gina's drinks, and she loads them onto her tray and leaves.

"Can I buy you a drink?" The guy next to me asks.

I was going to refuse when I felt his interest earlier because he's not my type, but what the hell? I am literally sipping sparkling ice water because every dollar in my purse is earmarked for rent. I have an eviction notice posted on my apartment door that I need to take care of before the time runs out and I'm out on the street. After my conversation with Gina, it seems like maybe I should let a guy treat me for once.

"Yeah, okay. I'll have a Moscow mule."

He flags down the bartender, and I get served right away because the guy knows I'm Gina's friend.

"What's your name?" He has to shout over the music which has been turned up as the club transitions from lounge to nightclub with the later hour.

"Lexi," I tell him.

"I'm Jayden." He holds his hand out, and I shake it. It's sweaty, and the handshake is awkward.

Ugh. I'm already regretting accepting the drink if it means I'm stuck making weird small talk with a stranger for the rest of my time here.

"What do you do?"

"I'm a hairstylist." I look around to see where Gina might be. How long before she can come over and rescue me. But the place is filling up. She's busy working the tables along the walls that are filled with new customers. She probably won't get much time to hang out with me tonight. "How about you?"

"I'm in sales."

Sales could mean anything at all. He could be a sign spinner on the corner. I doubt he's selling anything too spectacular based on the way he's dressed and carries himself. I'm not judging, just observing. I'm not one to poke holes in anyone else's financial situation when mine is so shitty. Still, this guy does nothing at all for me. I struggle through the chit chat while I suck down my drink which is mostly ice, anyway, and set it on the bar.

Jayden waves at the bartender to get me one more, but I shake my head. "I'm good, thanks." I slide off the barstool I was camped on. If I don't move from this spot, I won't be able to shake this guy.

"Thank you for the drink. I'm going to head out."

"What? You can't leave now, things are just warming up here."

I pull a mock mournful face. "I know, but I'm working tomorrow. Have to get my beauty rest."

He catches my arm. I grit my teeth to keep from shaking off his touch. "One more drink," he wheedles.

"Nah, I'm good. Thank you, though. It was nice talking to you."

Unfortunately, the bartender arrives with my drink, not catching or ignoring that I didn't want it.

"He already brought your drink. Now you have to stay." He flashes a smile that I'm sure is supposed to be charming.

I suck at situations like this. I really do. I was raised to be a good girl. Always be nice and polite. Never hurt anyone's feelings or insult them. Always smile. It makes it hard to figure out how to say no when someone's being pushy.

So I lie. "Yeah, okay. I'm just going to go to the bathroom," I say. Call me a chicken. It's true. "I'll be right back."

I walk toward the back of the club and pop into the women's room—that part wasn't a lie. Just the coming back part. I exit and head toward the back door. It's an emergency-only exit, but I can probably talk the bouncer stationed there into opening it for me since I'm Gina's friend, and I know Leo.

Except I'm stopped when fingers close around my arm, and Jayden yanks me backward.

"Ouch!" I glare at my unwanted suitor who apparently thinks he has a right to be pissed off now.

"Where are you going?" he demands, like I just screwed him out of five hundred bucks or a trip to Paris or something.

I open and shut my mouth trying to figure out if I'm going to tell the truth or fib again. I guess the jig is up.

I try to pull my arm away from him, but he hangs on. "I really have to go."

"I bought you two drinks," he accuses. Apparently, I owe him my firstborn child now.

"That was your choice. I didn't ask you to. In fact, I

tried to refuse the second one. Now let go." I yank harder. This guy is going to leave finger bruises on my arm.

"Bullshit, I heard you telling your friend you wanted a sugar daddy."

I'm not having this conversation. "Let go of me."

If anything, he squeezes tighter. I'm about to make a scene in hopes the bouncer at the door will notice and throw this guy out when a different hero shows up to save the day. A very well-dressed Italian hero.

"Let go of her." The guy seizes Jayden by the throat and shoves him up against the wall. Jayden lets go and stays pinned there, the side of his face mashed against the plaster.

"This guy bothering you?" my rescuer growls in a gruff, gravelly rumble. He's an extremely hot, older man with a commanding presence. One of the owners, then.

A mob boss.

The good girl, the nice girl in me would say no. Because complaining about people isn't polite. But I'm way too pissed. I rub the red marks on my arm where he held me. "Yeah."

My rescuer turns his attention to Jayden. "When a woman says *no*, you back the fuck off. *Capisce?*"

"Is there a problem, Mr. Manghini?" *Now* the bouncer appears. He's just as beefy and tattooed as Leo, but it's the mob boss–Mr. Manghini–who still seems to be the most dangerous man in the room.

"You need me to give you a lesson in manners?" Mr. Manghini asks. When Jayden doesn't answer, he shakes him by the throat. "Huh?"

"No." Jayden still sounds petulant, but his face is turning red from lack of oxygen, so I do think he's getting the message.

Mr. Manghini snorts and releases my stalker, shoving

him at the bouncer. "Throw him out. He was assaulting a customer." Then he holds up a hand and looks to me. "Unless you want to file charges?"

I'm shaky all over, but other than bruises on my arm, fine. "No." I start to say, "It's okay," but bite my tongue. It's not okay. Why would I even say that?

The bouncer hauls Jayden away and throws him out the back door, and Mr. Manghini gently slides his palm over the skin I'm rubbing. His fingers are large. They look strong. I'll bet he could've choked the life out of Jayden with just that one hand if he wanted.

For some reason, I find myself wondering what else he can do with those hands. What it would be like to have those commanding hands on my body in an altogether different way.

"You're hurt." His warm brown gaze circles my face. He smells like scotch and cigars, but it's not unpleasant. "And you're shaking. I'm sorry that happened to you here. Let me get you a drink to calm your nerves."

You'd think after what just happened, I'd never let another man buy me a drink, but there's something completely different about this guy's vibes. Somehow I'm sure that he wouldn't be douchy enough to think a drink buys him sex, and he obviously believes *no means no*. "Thanks, I..." I nod my head. "I'd like that."

"I'm Bobby." He extends a hand.

"Lexi." I place my hand in his, which is warm and strong. In fact, that's the energy he radiates–warm strength. To me, anyway. To Jayden, it was hard and cold. Ruthless, even. Bobby stands at least six feet tall, with broad shoulders perfectly draped in an Armani suit. I would guess him to be in his mid to late forties, with a strong jaw and aquiline nose. Dark eyes with lashes that curl.

He lightly touches my back to guide me back toward the bar.

The door that leads to the private lounge swings open. "Bobby, you coming back?" another man in a suit calls from the door.

"No." Bobby doesn't look away from me when he says it.

It's a weird feeling to have someone's full and complete attention. I try to sort out why it seems different from the attention Jayden gave me back at the bar. Jayden's attention felt intrusive, whereas this guy's makes me tingle all over. Like my cells are coming alive just from being in his presence.

"Are you the owner?" I ask as he escorts me through the clogged hallway that leads to the bar area.

"Nah, it's my cousin's place. My company built the building, though."

"Ah. Too bad, I was going to ask for a job." I adjust my purse strap on my shoulder.

His brows pop. "Yeah? You need a job, doll?" Again his scrutiny is intense. It's not sexual, but my body responds sexually. Heat pools between my legs. My nipples harden and tingle.

"A second job," I admit. "I have a day job, but I'd love to pick up a few evening or weekend shifts to get by."

Stan comes over. "Another mule?"

"Yeah. Sorry, I left that last one."

"What can I get you, Mr. Manghini?"

"Glen Livet on the rocks," Gina answers for him, appearing beside us. "This is the guy I was telling you about." She bumps my hips with hers, and I want the earth to open up and swallow me.

"Yeah?" Bobby searches my face, then hers. "What did

you say?"

"I just wanted you two to meet." Gina's smile is mischievous. I imagine she thinks of herself as the Sugar Daddy Cupid.

Is there such a thing? There totally should be.

"I feel like you two might hit it off."

Clearly, Bobby doesn't fall for bullshit because he narrows his eyes and cocks his head. "No, really."

"Lexi needs a sugar daddy."

"Oh my God." I clap a hand over my eyes like if I can't see Bobby, he can't see me. "I'm going to go jump off a tall building."

Bobby pries my fingers off my face. "You want a sugar daddy?" He looks amused.

"I didn't say that. This is all Gina's fantasy. I asked for a job–remember?"

His smile is warm. "I might be in the market for that situation."

Situation. I gasp when I suddenly realize what this is. "Oh no." I shake my head and take a step back. "I don't date married guys."

He holds up the back of his left hand to show me there's no ring. "Not married. I did that once. I'm not doing it again."

"Oh." I'm breathing hard like we're walking fast, even though we're standing still. "I'm not a prostitute," I blurt the next fear that comes to my mind.

His lips quirk. "I didn't think you were." He hands me my drink when it arrives. He's still considering me. "Sounds like you just need someone to spoil you a little. Is that right, doll?"

Spoil me.

Literally, no one has ever spoiled me in my entire life.

I've dated players and cheaters. They cared more about themselves and what I could do for them than vice versa.

I'm not saying I've bought into this idea of Gina's to pimp myself out for a sugar daddy, but the idea is definitely growing on me. Especially, or maybe only, because Bobby is the man in question.

Not that I think he would even want me. I mean, I don't know how this works. Is there a sign-up sheet somewhere? A way to put my name in for the position? Maybe he requires a resume outlining my best features. Recommendations, perhaps, from a past lover. Something like, *Gives great head, but a little needy*.

I realize he's waiting for an answer. I lick my lips. "Yeah, maybe," I admit. Oh God. I must be blushing. My face feels about fifty degrees too hot.

"That's *definitely* what she needs," Gina vouches for me. *Way to lay it right out there, girl.* She sure isn't one to beat around the bush.

"And Lexi's amazing. A good person. No drama. Would do anything for a friend. She's a very talented hairstylist, too."

"I'm not sure those are the qualities he's looking for in, um, his...whatever," I mumble.

Bobby chuckles.

He pulls a twenty-dollar bill from his pocket and offers it to the person who has taken the bar stool I occupied earlier. "Your drinks are on me if you give the lady your seat," he says.

I try to deny how pleasurable it is to have this guy focused on taking care of me. How long has it been since someone–anyone–has looked after me?

Oh yeah, never. My mom worked twelve-hour shifts as a nurse when I was growing up, so my sister and I were latch-key kids. My dad lived in Pittsburgh, so we weren't with him all that much, and even then, he lived with his girlfriend and her kids, so his focus was on them.

The guy grabs the twenty and vacates the seat, and Bobby puts his hands on my waist and lifts me onto it. When I'm settled, he keeps his hands there and gives me a wink. I feel it in my core, my belly fluttering, the muscles of my pelvic floor lifting. Okay, wow. I'm definitely feeling a connection.

Gina takes her tray of drinks and disappears with a smirk.

Bobby's gaze snags on the reddened marks on my arm from Jayden's fingers, and he scowls, brushing the backs of his fingers over my skin again. "I should've killed that guy for touching you."

A shiver runs across my skin because I suspect he means it. That he's murdered before.

I should be scared. Or at least put-off. Civilized men don't resort to violence.

But I'm not.

I'm turned on.

***

Bobby

Lexi shivers a bit, but her nipples protrude through her top like she's turned on.

The girl is smoking hot. She has sleek brown hair with glints of gold and mahogany, cut in the latest style, so it falls in soft wavy layers around her face. High cheekbones and big blue eyes give her an alluring beauty.

"So you do hair?"

Lexi nods. She's attentive, her eyes on me like she's

eager to please. It makes my dick thicken in my pants.

"No wonder you look so good."

She doesn't seem put off by my come-on-strong style. I definitely want her—at least for the night. I was sizing her up from the moment I heard that *stronzo* in the back say she was looking for a sugar daddy. Knowing what a girl wants makes negotiations so much clearer. Infinitely easier. I know if she wants a sugar daddy, she's willing to give me what I want, too.

The reins. Control.

She'll let me call the shots.

It's a clean arrangement—exactly what I'm looking for.

I can already tell she's a nice girl. My crazy-radar is on now after Stacy, but␖exi's not registering on it.

She was appropriately mortified when Gina suggested an arrangement between us and quick to let me know she didn't make this a practice. She doesn't sell her body for money. Still, she needs money, that's clear. She was looking for a side job at Swank.

Having a sugar daddy is a low-key arrangement. There's money involved, but it's more of a patronage or honorarium than a direct payment. I get to play generous, and she plays grateful, but we don't have an actual sex contract.

"This is really embarrassing. Did it seem like Gina was pimping me out? I swear that's not why I'm here."

My lips quirk. There, she just proved what I already suspected.

"But you're interested?" I ask.

She blinks, her lips parting. "Um…" She gives a husky laugh. "In having a sugar daddy? Or in you? Or–" she breaks off with an embarrassed laugh. "I'm not sure what I'm answering. Is there a position I apply for?" She's flirting now, leaning forward in her chair, her short skirt riding up her hips to give me a view of those creamy thighs. One of her knees has a long surgical scar down the inside that looks recent.

I step in closer. Damn, if she doesn't part her knees to let me stand between them. Fuck, if I don't want to get between them in a far more intimate way. I lower my head, hands resting on her thighs. "Let's start with a kiss. Are you interested in that?" I'm dying to taste her.

A little puff of air leaves her lips. She lifts her face to mine, lengthening her slender neck. I spy a tiny sunburst tattoo behind her ear, delicate and tasteful like her. "Yeah."

I go in slowly, brushing my lips across hers to start. When she chases the kiss, I deepen it, meeting her soft pillowy lips, stroking across them with mine. She moves hers in response, slips her tongue through to tease.

My dick gets hard. I clasp the back of her head and claim her mouth fully, my tongue penetrating the seam of her lips, gently fucking her mouth. She tastes like ginger ale and lime.

She moans softly. I need to get her out of here. I want her on a bed where I can fully explore her sweetness.

Her lids flutter open. "Was that part of the audition?"

This girl. So damn cute.

I cradle one side of her face and kiss her again–sweetly this time. "Yeah."

"How am I doing?" She looks up at me from under long lashes, her blue eyes darkened with desire.

"Let's just say I'm ready to move on to the next phase of the interview."

Her lips lift at the corners. "What does that entail?"

I tip my head toward the front doors. "Want to get out of here?"

Lexi holds my gaze for a beat then slides forward. I

catch her hips to help her hop down off the bar stool. Picking up her purse, I hand it to her as I wrap an arm behind her waist to escort her out.

She catches Gina's eye on the way out, and her friend gives her a thumbs up.

"Do you have a car here? I ask, thinking we can drive together in her ride, so she feels like she has control over when she can leave.

"Um, no. I'm kind of between cars right now." I detect embarrassment in her rueful laugh. She's damn cute. "Where are we going, anyway?"

"The Four Seasons."

Her eyebrows rise, and I know I impressed her.

"Come on." I lead her to my new electric Porsche and hold the door for her to hand her in. When I open the door on my side, I hear her muttering *this is craz–*. She breaks off and sends me a crooked smile.

I climb in and start up the car. "Are you nervous, doll?"

"Um, a little."

"Don't worry babygirl, this isn't a real audition. It's just a test of chemistry."

"I just...I'm not sure what you're expecting."

Everything about this girl is disarming. She's so genuine. Honest. It's refreshing.

"I'm expecting you'll share that hot little body of yours with me. You don't have to perform. I like to be in charge in bed."

Understatement.

"I'll take what I want. If I need something from you, I'll let you know."

She relaxes, which is a good sign. She wants me to lead. I thought I picked up submissive tendencies from her, and it seems I was right.

"Don't worry. If you tell me to back off at any point, I will. I come on strong, and I play a little rough, but I know how to treat a lady."

Her azure eyes search mine as if trying to decipher what I mean by *playing rough*. I lean over and brush my lips across hers, wanting to taste her full raspberry lips again.

"I'm also expecting I'll make you scream. In a good way."

She laughs, a throaty, sensual sound that goes straight to my cock. "Oh really? I guess you don't lack confidence, do you?"

"Nope." I deliberately hold her gaze.

Her pupils dilate. "What if I'm one of those women who never orgasms with a partner?"

I rake my gaze down her body again, wondering what kind of assholes she's dated who couldn't worship that body well enough to make her come. "Is that the case?"

She swallows and shrugs. Now I'm determined to make her forget every cock-sucker she ever let touch that juicy body of hers.

"Then I'll figure out how to unlock your secrets." I gun my Porsche to surge into the gap in traffic, and Lexi gasps, white-knuckling the dashboard.

"You okay, doll?" I glance over. "Does my driving make you nervous?"

She lets out a shaky laugh and eases her hands away from the dash. "Sorry. It's not your driving. I just get jumpy on the road. This city has some crazy drivers."

I remember her "between cars" embarrassment and wonder if there's a story there. I'm about to ask when she changes the subject. "Were you born here?"

"In New Jersey? Or America? Either way, yeah. First generation American."

"Your parents are from Italy?"

I know what she's trying to figure out. Whether I'm in *La Cosa Nostra*—the mafia. Or maybe she already knows and is curious about it. "Yeah. Sicily."

"Are they still around?" She darts a glance at me. "I'm sorry—do you mind my asking personal questions?"

I don't think she's a plant fishing for information, but you never know. I would sure hate to find that out because she's far too beautiful to destroy.

"I don't mind this question. Some I might." I soften the words with quirked lips. "Both my parents are dead, but I have a ton of extended family."

She nods.

"As a rule, the Family is off-limits for conversation. For your safety and mine." I pull into the parking garage for the Four Seasons and find a spot.

"Yeah, okay." As she bobs her head, a slight tremor runs through her, and I hope I haven't scared her off.

"Don't worry, Lex." I get out and walk around to open her door, but she climbs out before I reach it. "You're safe. If we strike an arrangement, my business won't ever concern you. That's the point of keeping it off-limits. *Capisce?*"

She nods. I cradle her nape and draw her face up to mine for another kiss. She softens into me, her lips supple and receptive, her body melting into mine.

Taking her hand, I lead her to the lobby and ask for a luxury suite. The clerk gives me the keycard and directs us to the elevator. As soon as the door closes, I nudge her back against the wall, nuzzling and nipping at her neck.

"Still nervous?"

"No."

"Liar." I murmur in her ear.

Chapter Three

Lexi

I try not to look too impressed at the gorgeous luxury hotel suite, which is twice as big as my apartment. It has a separate living room, complete with a marble fireplace and ten-foot floor-to-ceiling windows overlooking the city. I stand at the window and look down, awed.

Bobby grasps my nape and pulls me close, kissing the side of my neck.

I'm not afraid of him, but I am nervous. It's more performance anxiety. I don't know what I'm doing. What he wants. How this works.

He presses the backs of his fingers over my heart, and it thumps to meet them, betraying my anxiety.

"I never do this sort of thing," I admit.

"I know," he murmurs, his expression soft. "That's one of the things I like about you."

"What else do you like?" I'm not above fishing for compliments.

He picks up a section of my hair and runs it over his

cheek. "Everything I've seen so far." His voice is low and seductive. "I'm going to have a hard time holding back." He traces my collarbone with the tip of his finger.

"Then maybe you shouldn't" I whisper.

He smiles like a satisfied cat and leads me down the hall, his hand at the small of my back like a gentleman.

Once inside, he yanks my body against his, kissing me hard. I moan against his mouth, loving the way he takes charge. He sweeps his tongue between my lips, claiming my mouth. Owning me. His hands knead my ass, then he drags them upward, peeling the fabric of my dress from my body in a single sweep.

"Mmm." He stands back and drinks in my black and hot pink satin bra and matching panties. "I like those."

Thank God he didn't catch me in my cotton Wonder Woman panties with the holes worn at the seams. Every inch of my skin heats under his dark gaze. I start to kick off my heels, but he shakes his head.

I freeze, waiting for more information.

All he says is, "Good girl."

My pussy clenches in response. Apparently, I have a praise kink.

"You look so beautiful in nothing but those heels," he rumbles approvingly. He slips a finger under each strap of my bra and peels the cups down slowly to reveal my breasts.

He drinks them in, appreciation evident, then he grows impatient again, yanking the bra to my waist, and crushing a hand over one of my breasts as his mouth bends to the other. He flicks his tongue over the tip of my nipple, then sucks it deep into his mouth before releasing it abruptly and nipping with his teeth.

I gasp, clawing at his arms at the brief pain he inflicted before he returns to pleasuring me. My internal muscles squeeze and clench. He moves so fast and with such confidence, he overwhelms my senses, and I melt into his touch. He strokes one hand down my belly, slipping inside the front of my panties where he brushes a finger across my dripping pussy. The shock of touch on my most sensitive parts makes me moan.

"Someone's wet," he murmurs approvingly, the deep rich tones of his voice reverberating through every sinew of my body. He yanks my panties down then pushes me back onto the bed. Hoisting my legs into the air, he holds my ankles with one hand and gives my ass a slap.

I gasp in surprise, squirming against the grip he already loosed to unbuckle his belt and kick off his pants and boxer briefs. I stare when he pulls off his shirt to reveal a broad, muscled chest dusted with dark curls. My eyes slide lower, where his cock juts out proudly, his erection impressive. I lick my lips, my heart skittering. No wonder he has confidence in his bedroom performance.

Despite the fact that he already knows I'm wet, he pushes my legs wide and settles between them, licking into me. I cry out at the contact, then go cross-eyed with pleasure because the man has zero trouble finding his way around my clit. He circles it with his tongue, flicks it, and somehow even manages to suck it between his lips. He rubs it with his thumb while he pushes into me with two other fingers. When he finds my G-spot and pumps against it, I screech with a surprise orgasm. My internal muscles clench around his fingers, and I squirt a little, which would've embarrassed me, except he chuckles. "That's it, doll."

He eases his fingers out and climbs off the bed. "You don't usually orgasm with a partner, or you don't orgasm during intercourse?" When he reappears, he has a condom in hand, which he rips open with his teeth.

"Neither...both." My brain cells are too occupied with my pleasure centers to know how to answer the question.

"I'd say the problem was with your partner." He kneels on the bed and sheaths his length. "Put those sexy heels over my shoulders."

It's bossy, but I don't take offense. In fact, I love how he knows exactly what he wants and asks for it. It makes it easy for me to just be present. I lift my legs in the air, careful not to kick him in the face.

He wastes no time in lining his cock up with my entrance and pushing in. He's thick and long, filling me. Stretching me. When he grips the front of my thighs to yank my ass against him, thrusting into the hilt, I cry out at the unexpected pleasure.

He stays in deep to let me adjust, groaning his own satisfaction. "You okay, doll?"

"So good," I manage to pant.

He withdraws and repeats the action, his loins slapping against my ass. He picks up speed. "Yeah, I knew you'd be a hot fuck." His dirty talk revs my engine, the deep rumble turning my insides to liquid heat. "You're a perfect, sexy, willing little fuck doll, aren't you?"

I can't answer, not that I think he expects me to. I suddenly find myself not just wanting and willing but rather desperate to be exactly that–his willing little fuck doll. To have this man as my boss in bed. My sugar daddy. Not for the money. For this.

The pleasure. The sense of surrender to someone who knows exactly what he's doing. How he wants it. How to make it good for me. His rough domination stokes my internal fire hotter.

I swear the entire room has caught fire. I've never felt so abandoned. So willingly out of control. It's a hard fuck–

aggressive, pounding–and yet my body opens like a flower to him, not just willing to give whatever he demands but deriving intense pleasure from those demands.

Orgasming with him seems to be a non-issue. I'm already close to a second one, about to break, when he pulls out. "Flip over," he commands gruffly.

I laugh softly, not used to being ordered around during sex. I had no idea it would be such a turn-on. My role here is a sexual servant–which is somehow freeing. All the repression I've had in the past, the performance anxiety about doing it right, or whether I look good naked, or whatever the stupid thoughts going around in my head were– they're all gone.

Bobby's in charge. All I have to do is surrender to him.

Still, I lodge my complaint. "I was just about to come."

"I know."

Cocky bastard. The two simple words shoot me into a dizzying state of lust. He knew. He guaranteed my satisfaction back at the club, and despite what seemed like a self-centered encounter, he *is* paying attention. My limbs tremble as I turn around, climbing further up the bed to lie on my belly. He grabs my thighs and yanks me back toward him, my feet finding the floor in a spread eagle, my ass presented to him. A cry of need erupts as he feeds his hard cock into my slick channel and pumps. When he grasps both my shoulders to brace me for his pounding, I lose control. "Oh, God, oh yes, please!" I sob into the bedcovers.

"Not yet, *cara mia*. Wait for permission."

Wait...what?

"You don't come until I tell you."

There's that bossy tone again. His cocky dictates. I shouldn't love it so much, but I do. It's like he knows some secret about sex or this encounter that I don't. He has a plan. He's the master of the scene.

I breathe hard, trying to hold off the impending orgasm that shimmers and simmers right at the brink.

"Please?" I pant. I swear I don't think I can hold it off any longer.

He continues slamming into me, his balls swinging to tap my clit, the head of his cock driving deep.

"Now, *bambina*. Come now, sweetheart."

The moment he commands it, I come.

"Yeah!" he roars, slamming his cock deep inside me as he comes. My pussy squeezes around his cock, as wave after wave of release flows through me.

My mind goes blank, and I enjoy the sensation of complete surrender and satisfaction.

After a few moments, Bobby brings me back, easing out of me and murmuring, "Thank you, Lexi. That was hot." He strokes his hand down the length of my back, his touch light.

"Mmm," I moan, too relaxed to move.

He kisses my nape and moves away. I float again until the sensation of a warm washcloth between my thighs brings me back to the moment. I'm surprised at the gesture, but maybe I shouldn't be.

Despite his roughness in bed, Bobby is the caretaking type. He took care of me at the club, and he took care of me here. Even during the sex, he was an extremely sensitive lover, completely in tune with me. I wonder what he would've done if he'd found me dry and tense, as sometimes happens when I get nervous about sex. Would he have taken the time to learn how to unlock my secrets as he claimed? It seems like he already knows them because he just revealed something about me I hadn't known: I like being used. Commanded.

Maybe Gina was right all along. A sugar daddy is exactly what I need.

"Kick off your shoes now," he murmurs and pulls down the covers of the bed.

I obey, and he slides an arm under my knees to lift me onto the bed, climbing over me. As if to prove my theory, he's careful to pull my hair out from under my shoulders.

He kisses me roughly. "I'm definitely keeping you, doll."

* * *

Bobby

When Lexi stiffens, I have to remind myself that I can't always say all the dominant possessive things in my head to a woman. Especially not one I just met, no matter how submissive and willing she may seem.

I do want her, though. I want to keep her in my spare apartment and treat her like a princess and a sex slave. Tie her up, spank her, spoil her with nice things. I want those eager-to-please eyes on my face while she's on her knees, her mouth stretched around my cock.

I could probably move in for the kill right now. It sounded like she needed cash rather urgently. But I don't want to coax her into something that makes her nervous, even though I easily could. I want her to be the one offering.

So I pull the covers up and kiss her forehead. "Stay here tonight, doll. Order up room service in the morning. Buy yourself something nice from the gift shop and charge it to the room." I get dressed and drop a wad of bills on the dresser. There's probably three or four hundred dollars there. I don't count it because I don't want her to feel cheap.

I'm not paying for sex. Sugar daddies don't pay for sex, they provide support in exchange for the privilege of ownership.

"This is for you to treat yourself tomorrow," I tell her. "If you decide you want a sugar daddy, you know where to find me."

I leave it at that. I don't get her number. Don't leave her mine.

I hope to see her again, but I'm not gonna push.

She leans up on her elbows, her breasts separating. It's damn hard not to crawl back in bed and kiss that space between them. Follow it up to her neck and behind her ear.

But no, she's skittish. I've already come on strong. If I stay, she might tuck her tail and run in the morning. Better to let her come to me when she's ready.

Either she wants to be owned or she doesn't.

I strongly suspect she'll realize she does.

I hope so. Because Lexi seems absolutely perfect for me.

Chapter Four

Lexi

This morning, I woke in the luxury hotel suite with my body sore in all the right places. I ordered room service. Bought myself a swimsuit at the gift shop and sat in the hot tub. Lived it up. It was *ah-mazing*.

Bobby left me over four hundred dollars to "treat" myself. Sadly, the only treat I'll get is paying off the rent I owe. I didn't have time to run back to my apartment to find the building manager and pay it off before work. At this point, what difference does it make when he gets the money–Saturday or Sunday? I'll get it to him before Monday. That's all that matters.

Right now, I have a just-for-me hair project to work on. It's after hours, and everyone's gone except for Ondrea, the receptionist.

"So you're letting me do anything I want, right?" I push Gina into my salon chair. I offered her a free cut and color if she would model for my portfolio.

She tosses her dark hair over one shoulder. "Yes. I trust you. But only if you tell me everything about last night."

"Ooh, what happened last night?" Ondrea instantly appears behind me, clacking her lacquered nails together. She's an adorable trans woman, who is barely out of high school and full of sass. She is literally the best thing about renting at Stylz because she has that knack for making everything fun and entertaining.

"I hooked up with a guy." I flick a cape around Gina's shoulders. I already have a plan in mind, so I begin to mix the hair dye in plastic bowls.

"A potential sugar daddy." Gina waggles her brows.

"Ooh. Tell me more." Ondrea flops into the empty salon chair beside Gina's.

"Yeah. Spill, girl."

"So, first of all, you missed how I met him. He literally saved me from Mr. sugar daddy wannabe idiot back by the bathrooms." I finish mixing the dye and start combing through Gina's hair.

"What do you mean?" she asks.

I separate the first section of hair and paint the color on it, then fold it up in foil. "The guy who bought me drinks thought that meant I owed him something, and he was trying to drag me back to the bar or something. Bobby grabbed him by the throat and smashed his face against the wall."

Ondrea gives an exaggerated gasp. "Hawt."

"Super hot," Gina agrees.

"I know. And then I find out he's your big tipper, so it sort of seemed meant to be." I work the next section into foil, having long ago mastered the trick of keeping up a conversation and applying hair color.

"Sooo?" Gina drags out the "o" with a lift of her brows.

I nod my head as if I'm answering a yes or no question. "He was hot."

"That's it? I want details."

"Yeah, we want details." Ondrea spins the salon chair around in circles.

"Well, he took me to the Four Seasons, went down on me, fucked me hard, and tucked me in for the night."

Ondrea pauses spinning to fan herself with her fingers, her tastefully long false lashes fluttering.

"Wait–so he didn't stay?" Gina's dissected my report already.

"No. Are you sure he's not married?"

"Uh oh," Ondrea says. "I don't like that."

"He's not. He's just playing sugar daddy. I'm telling you–that's his thing. This is why you need him." Gina taps her finger on the arm of her chair to make her point.

"I don't know." I shrug. I loved last night–don't get me wrong. But it sort of felt like a relief when he left. I was feeling like I was in over my head and getting worried about what I was getting myself into. Especially when he said, *I'm keeping you.* I don't even know what he meant by that, but it scared me a little.

"Don't know what? Was he good in bed?"

Understatement. "So good."

"Then what aren't you sure about?" Ondrea wants to know.

"I'm not going to enter into some kind of financial arrangement for sex. I'm just not. That seems crazy."

"The oldest profession." Ondrea stands from her chair. "It's not wrong to receive money just for being you. Just for being someone's entertainment. It's not like you hated it."

"Yeah, I don't know."

"Well, how did he leave it? Is he going to call? What's the deal?" Gina presses.

"Actually, he didn't even ask for my number, but he said if I'm interested, I know where to find him."

"So stew on it."

Ondrea comes over to observe my technique closer. "Are you doing the same thing with her that you did with me?" I did her hair last week for photos for the portfolio, putting some dramatic fuchsia streaks around her face and underneath in the back.

"No, I'm going with something a little more subtle. Shades of burgundy."

"Why do you need new portfolio pictures?" Gina asks.

"I'm applying for a training job with Stellar Hair Color. If I get it, they will fly me all over the country to teach hair stylists how to use their dyes."

"Ooh, that sounds glamorous."

"I know, and the pay is $120,000 a year."

"Wow!"

"Which means I probably have no chance." I paint another section of Gina's hair.

"Don't say that. You deserve that kind of salary. You're worth it."

"I'm thinking about filing bankruptcy to clear my medical bills," I confide because I honestly cannot pin my hopes on this job. Bankruptcy won't help with the back pay for the apartment or the salon, but if I could get out from under the medical debt, I could breathe a little.

"Don't tell Arissa that," Ondrea warns. "She's already freaking out because you're behind on rent here." Arissa is the salon owner. I'll admit that paying her took a slightly lower priority to paying the rent on my apartment, but I'd like to think she knows I'm good for it. I mean, I'm here every day, working my ass off. She knows I'm trying.

"I'm going to pay it just as soon as I get my landlord

paid off," I say, in case Ondrea repeats this conversation to Arissa.

"I have two words for you," Gina says, and I roll my eyes because I know what's coming. "Sugar. Daddy."

* * *

Bobby

"Mr. Manghini?" Greta, my secretary, calls me at the construction site.

"What is it?" She knows I don't like to be bothered when I'm in the field, so the fact that she's calling means something else has gone wrong.

"There's an IRS auditor here. He's demanding to review all your bookkeeping."

Fanculo.

I grit my teeth. "Did you ask for identification?"

"Yes. He seems legit." Greta has worked for me for sixteen years. She's in the Family–the older sister of one of our soldiers–and therefore someone I trust. Not that I ever let her become a party to anything. She's innocent, yet in the know, generally-speaking, which makes her an ideal employee as far as I'm concerned.

"Okay. Show him whatever he wants to see."

"Are you sure?"

My books are tight. I may launder Family money through the business, but the paper trail is impeccable. They won't find anything.

"I'm sure. Nothing to worry about at all."

"Totally sure?"

"Greta, I appreciate your concern, but there's nothing to be worried about. It's fine."

"All right. I will let him see the accounting."

I end the call and dial the don. Even though it's not going to be a problem, he wouldn't like me keeping him in the dark about anything that involves the government sniffing around our affairs.

"Bobby. You're interrupting my golf game," he says when he picks up.

"Then I won't keep you. Just wanted to let you know I have an IRS auditor demanding to see my books. Nothing to worry about."

Al's silent for a moment. Long enough to make me sweat his reaction. "Okay. Keep me posted."

"Yeah. Will do." I end the call and shove the phone in my pocket.

Cristo.

I sure as fuck hope things are as clean as I believe because if I bring anything down on the LaTorre family, prison time will be the least of my worries.

* * *

Lexi

I walk from the bus stop to my apartment, my feet aching from standing all day. I have eleven hundred and fifty dollars cash in my pocket, a combination of the money Bobby gave me and my earnings this week, which I hope is enough to get the eviction notice off my door. I unlock the front door to the building and take the stairs up to the third floor, so I can eat a bite of food before I find the building manager.

I try my key in the lock.

It doesn't work.

Fuck! This can't be. I try again, gripping the doorknob

to rattle the door as I try to jam the key in. But the inner portion of the lock is obviously new.

I've been officially evicted. I should have come by this morning instead of hanging out in the hot tub at the Four Seasons. I should have at least called the landlord to tell him I had a partial payment.

Maybe it's not too late.

I race down the stairs, tears burning in my eyes. How stupid could I be, to think I could keep talking my landlord out of booting me? I should've moved home with my mom after the accident and paid the bills down over time. Instead, I hid my head in the sand and just hoped things would work out.

Well, they didn't work out.

And now I have no place to go.

I wipe my face when I get to the manager's door.

Get it together, Lex.

I draw a breath, pull out my cash and knock on the door.

The manager, a decent middle-aged guy named Gus, answers. "I'm sorry, Lexi." He looks away.

I thrust the money at him. "This is eleven hundred and fifty dollars. That covers this month, at least, and I can work on chipping down the debt on the rest. I'm so sorry. I meant to come by this morning to give this to you, but I slept somewhere else and didn't have time before work, but–"

"Sorry." He shakes his head. I think he actually does regret turning me away. "It's not up to me. I just do what I'm told, and I was told to change the locks."

"No, no, no, no." I'm talking fast like it's going to make some kind of difference. "Please, Gus. Can you just let me in there for tonight, and I'll call the landlord in the morning to get it all paid off? I'm sure he'd rather keep an existing tenant and get the money he's owed rather than find a new renter."

"That is not true. He's bumping the rent to sixteen hundred, and he says he has three people on the waiting list for it. I'm sorry, Lexi, but it's too late. You're out."

I try to hold in a sob, pinching my lips together as a couple of tears leak from the outer corners of my eyes. "Can you just let me in to get my stuff?"

"I can't, Lexi."

"Just a few essential things? An overnight bag? Who will know?"

"Not until I hear it from the landlord. Call him first thing in the morning and make arrangements to get your stuff. I'll open the door when he gives me the okay."

I press my lips together tight and nod, more tears falling.

Gus shuts the door in my face–not like he doesn't care, but more like he's sorry, and seeing me cry sucks for him. I almost wish he was more of a dick, so I could be mad at anyone besides myself for this situation.

Dammit! I totally fucked up. I have that "bad girl" feeling I always get when I mess something up. Shameful and small. Guilty.

Weak.

I run down the hall and out the door, heading back to the subway station. I take it to the stop closest to Swank. I can try to talk to the landlord tomorrow. Right now, I need a drink and a friend.

I wasn't even thinking about finding Bobby. I'm not the kind of girl with rescue fantasies because in my world, that shit doesn't come true.

But the moment I push through the door, a strong arm wraps around my waist and Bobby pulls me back against him. "Hold up there, doll. Is everything okay? Have you been crying?"

Even though last night the situation with Bobby stressed me out, something in me relaxes now.

I turn in his arms and fail at a smile. "Just a bad day. I could really use a drink."

"Let's get you one, then." Bobby takes my elbow in that take-charge way of his and leads me toward the bar. The moment we arrive, the bartender is there. "The usual, Mr. Manghini?"

"Yeah, and whatever Lexi wants. She's on my tab for the night. I want you to take very good care of her, understand?"

"Yes, sir."

"Two shots of Cazadores," I order.

Bobby raises his brows. "That bad?"

I try to wipe the misery from my face but probably don't manage.

"Listen, no strings with the drinks, baby," Bobby says in a low voice to me. "I had a great time last night, but there's no pressure. I get the feeling you didn't come here to see me tonight."

"No. I mean—"

"It's all right." His eyes crinkle. The bartender appears with our drinks, and he picks his up. "I'll give you some space."

"No, it's okay." I grab one shot and down it, biting into the lime to quench the shudder. "I just have to talk to Gina." I pick up the second shot, but Bobby places his hand over mine to stop me from downing it. "And then I would love to talk to you. I mean, if you wanted to talk. Oh." My face heats. "Maybe you don't want to talk." Maybe he just wants sex.

"Slow down, doll. Take a breath." He looks around. "Here comes your friend now."

Gina struts over, carrying her empty cocktail tray. It never ceases to amaze me that she can stand all night in three-inch heels, but as usual, she's rocking them with a short skirt.

"I'll let you two talk," Bobby says smoothly, leaving before I can answer.

"Hey, what are you doing here? I thought you were headed home."

Even in my crappy mood, I have to admire her new hairstyle. I did a kick-ass job with it, and she looks great. Hopefully, the photos will get me that job.

"I got evicted," I blurt as soon as I check to make sure Bobby's out of earshot. "I'm locked out. I feel like such a loser."

"Shit." She gives me a hug. "I'm sorry. Well, you can definitely crash on my couch."

"Thanks."

"Do you want the key now?"

I find myself searching the lounge for Bobby's broad shoulders. He's gone back to the high-top near the door where he must've been when I came in. There are a couple of younger guys there who also look like they belong in the Family with a capital F.

Our gazes lock across the club like he'd been waiting for me to look over. I raise my hand and give a shy wave.

"Mm...maybe after I've had a drink or two," I answer Gina without looking away from Bobby, who is now headed toward me. My entire body turns on like he's the electrical current, and I just got plugged in.

"Of course. Or maybe you'll find a better offer."

"I...That's not why I came here," I sputter like I'm

defending myself to some invisible person judging me right now. Of course, that invisible person is me.

"Let him take care of you. Is that so hard?"

"Shhh. He's coming over."

Bobby arrives, and Gina starts selling me again. "Lexi just gave me this cut and color." She shakes out her hair. "She did it for her portfolio."

Bobby raises his eyebrows as if he's genuinely interested. But he can't be. No guy ever gives a crap about what I do. "Oh yeah? What's the portfolio for?"

I nibble my lower lip. "I'm applying for this training job. It's posted nationally, so I probably don't have much of a chance, but it's worth a shot."

He nods. "Well, if all the styles in your portfolio look as good as yours and Gina's, I would say you do have a good chance. Not that I'm an expert on women's hair."

I like the way his eyes crinkle at the corners, the dark lashes making the brown liquid pools look warm and inviting. The way my belly flutters when he looks at me.

"Well, I'd better get back to work." Gina tucks her tray under her arm. "Are you both all set on drinks?"

I haven't touched the second shot yet. Bobby told me to slow down, and for some reason, it seems I want to please him. "I'm good, thanks."

"Me too."

I find myself leaning forward, wanting a whiff of Bobby's cologne. To feel the heat of his body. As if he knows, he steps closer.

"You two talk about the sugar daddy thing. I think it could work." Gina drops a wink before she departs.

Bobby considers me. "I'm all in, doll. I told you that last night. If you want to be spoiled a little, I'm your guy."

The flesh between my legs tugs upward. All the shame

and despair over getting evicted lifts away, is replaced by heat. Interest. Desire.

What do I have to lose, really? A sugar daddy could solve my immediate problems if this is for real. "What would your expectations be of me?"

His eyes darken, and he steps closer, draping an arm across the back of my barstool. "The mere fact that you asked tells me you're the right girl for me."

I try to decipher his meaning as my pulse races at his nearness. I catch the pleasant scent of his cologne, and it takes me back to the pleasure we shared last night.

"It's pretty simple, Lexi. I would expect you to be at my beck and call, available any time I please. That doesn't mean you won't have time to yourself. You will. I'm a busy man."

I swallow, my panties dampening at the idea of being his sexual servant. "And what exactly would you offer in return?"

Bobby's thumb lightly traces lines on my shoulder. "I've got a nice apartment where you can live. I'll take you out and treat you right. Give you spending cash. How does that sound?"

Our eyes lock. Heat pools in my core, traveling up until my face grows warm. My breath rises and falls in a rapid rhythm.

"Would I be living with you?"

"No, doll. I have my own place. It would be your pad. It's luxe—my company renovated the place, so it has all the bells and whistles. Jacuzzi bathtub. Big kitchen. Rooftop pool. Gym."

I'm getting lightheaded at the mere possibility. This really could solve all my problems. I mean, I'm literally homeless right now, and I may not even have access to any of my things if my ex-landlord is a dick about it.

I swallow. "I-I'd like that."

"Yeah?" His lids droop, and he slides his hand around my nape, stroking the sensitive skin there. "I'm glad. You seem perfect for me." He leans closer and speaks in a low, rumbling voice, "But you should know, I would use you however I want, whenever I want. And I demand fidelity. No other men."

"What about women?" I ask, just to see what he'll say.

He seems to know I'm testing. He quirks a smile. "Only if I get to watch."

* * *

Bobby

I kiss Lexi, cupping the back of her head to hold her in place. She responds, her lips soft and supple. When we pull apart, I settle beside her, stroking my hand up and down the curve of her hip. "So, Lexi, are you in some kind of trouble?"

She goes still. "What do you mean?"

"I get the feeling you wouldn't normally do something like this. Gina introduced us for a reason. I'm hoping it's not because you're an informer." I smirk when her eyes round because I'm already certain she's not.

She shakes her head.

"Something's put the pinch on you. What is it?"

She opens her mouth, but no words come out.

"Is it money? Are you running from someone? Do you need protection?"

She draws in a shaky breath. "No, not at all."

"Nah, don't lie to me, Lexi. That's gonna be a rule."

She blinks with wide eyes but doesn't speak.

"Tell me."

Tears form in those beautiful blue eyes. "I got evicted today," she admits, not quite meeting my gaze.

I nod, not surprised. I knew something had to be going on because she's definitely not your usual bar floozy out to sink her claws into a rich guy. Nor is she just in it for the sex. She seemed surprised by her response to me last night. No, Lexi seems like a smart, normal girl who's never done anything like this in her life. Which totally adds to her appeal. "Is your stuff still there, at your apartment?"

"Yeah. But I can't get in and get it."

I get up and fish my phone out of my trouser pocket. "What's the address?" I ask, my thumb poised over the keypad.

"Why?"

"Because I'm going to get it back for you." I raise my eyebrows to prompt her.

"3650 E. Walnut #254."

"Landlord's name and number?"

"Darrell Jones. I'll get his number." She pulls out her phone and scrolls through her contacts. "What are you going to do to him?"

I laugh. "What do you want me to do to him?"

"Nothing...I mean—"

I chuckle again. "I was just thinking along the lines of paying him enough to open up the place and let me move your stuff out."

"Oh." She looks embarrassed. "Sorry. I just...don't know how all this works."

"Did you think I was going to break his kneecaps?"

She shakes her head quickly in a way that tells me that's exactly what she thought.

"I'm just an ordinary guy, Lex." It's not exactly true, but

it's the story I maintain. "I work in real estate and new construction. I use Family contacts to make deals, and I'm not above bending the law a bit to avoid paying Uncle Sam more than his fair share, but I'm not a thug." *Unless I need to be.*

Her face flushes. "I'm sorry. I didn't mean to offend you."

"Come here." I pull her face up to mine and kiss her. "I'm not offended. I think you're cute."

She ducks her face by looking down at her phone to find the landlord's contact information, which she reads off to me.

I enter it into my phone, then give it to her. "Put your number in."

She sends herself a text that says, *This is Lexi.* "Thank you." She looks vulnerable. "I really appreciate it."

I put a knuckle under her chin to lift her pretty face. "I will handle all your problems. I always take care of what's mine," I promise.

"You want me to owe you."

I grin. "Smart girl."

The corners of her lips quirk, and my dick thickens. I have mad chemistry with this woman.

"I'll let you know how it goes with your landlord–whether I have to rearrange his face or not." She looks up, and I wink. "Just kidding. I mean, I could go that route if you want." I narrow my eyes, aggression suddenly flooding my veins at a thought. "*Did he touch you?* Hurt you?"

"No, no, no."

"Screw you over?"

She shakes her head quickly, and I force myself to relax. "It was my fault. I got behind on rent and stupidly thought he'd let me keep chipping away at the balance." She shrugs. "He didn't."

"Well, fuck him. You're gonna love your new place. I'll take you right now. Or as soon as you want."

She picks up her second shot of tequila, downs it, then hops off the barstool. "I'm ready."

I throw a hundred-dollar bill down on the bar for Stan, the bartender, and take her hand. I like that she's not as nervous with me this time. She seems relieved–like she trusts me to take care of her.

I will. I definitely want to take care of her and her problems because I can tell she doesn't deserve them.

***

Lexi

"So tell me about this job you're applying for," Bobby says in the car, surprising me with what seems like genuine interest.

"It's a trainer position for Stellar, a major hair product company. They're looking for a representative to teach workshops on how to use their hair color."

"Sounds great."

"Yeah, it's a great salary with benefits, but I don't know if I have a real shot at it or not."

"Why not?"

My face heats. "I don't know...I mean, my work is good, but–"

"But what?"

I shrug. "I don't know if it's good enough."

Bobby frowns. "No, fuck that," he says. "*Is* it good enough?" There's a demand in his voice, but it's not unkind. I can tell he's trying to coach me here.

I grow even hotter and shift in the Porsche's seat as I consider the question. Do I really believe my work is good enough for me to be hired? Do I think I deserve this position? "Yeah." I'm sort of surprised by my answer. "I'm good." Admitting it out loud feels sacrilegious but also wonderful. Like I'd been hiding how good I was from the world for fear of getting singled out. Or having someone smack me down and tell me I'm not. I nod, a bubbling sense of enthusiasm growing in my chest. "I'm really good."

Bobby grins. "Then own it, baby. You're fantastic, and you deserve this position."

I glance down at my hands clutching my purse in my lap. "I do."

"Good girl. Send your portfolio in with that attitude, and they'll hire you in a heartbeat."

I lean back in my seat, feeling more comfortable. "Thanks."

Bobby reaches over and squeezes my knees. "Don't thank me. It's all you, doll. You're the one with talent here."

As we drive, I sneak glances at him, remembering our sex the night before. I think of him naked--all chiseled muscle, dark, manly curls dusting his chest. Using him out of financial desperation isn't really a sacrifice. He doesn't seem like the kind who has to buy a lover. In fact, I'm surprised he doesn't have women throwing themselves at his feet. Of course, maybe he does...

Either way, it doesn't matter. This is a temporary situation, obviously. I won't get emotionally involved because it's not a real relationship. It's more like a job or a position. A position that might be easy because of the great boss.

He drives to his apartment and parks in an underground parking lot, leading me to the elevator with his hand at my low back. He kisses me on the way up, and I melt with each persistent stroke of his tongue. By the time we reach his floor, my skin tingles for his touch.

"So this is the place." Bobby tosses me the keys after he opens the door to his apartment. "The washer and dryer are in that closet over there. Garbage gets dumped in the bin in the parking garage. The cleaners come in every other Tuesday, around noon."

Cleaners? Um, wow. Hell, yes, I will live in a luxe apartment that comes with a bi-monthly cleaning service!

"The gym is on the top floor, and the pool is on the roof. Your door key opens both."

This is too good to be true. The high-rise apartment shines with posh polished hardwood floors, granite countertops, and gleaming stainless appliances. I never lived in any sort of luxury—my lower-middle-class Jersey upbringing and making ends meet as a hair stylist hasn't afforded such opulence.

I look around, imagining what it would be like to make this arrangement with Bobby long-term. To have this be my place. To settle into something semi-permanent with him.

Of course, that will never happen. But I'll receive right now.

I twist the keys around my thumb. "So I can stay here? You're giving me the keys, just like that?"

He steps closer, his hand settling on my waist. "Yeah. I like you, Lexi." He lowers his head. "You're hot as fuck. You're responsive as hell in bed. And my gut says you're a good person."

I wrinkle my brow. "But you don't even know me. Aren't you afraid I'll walk off with your television or something?"

He scoffs. "Nobody steals from Bobby Manghini."

The reality of his statement hits home. Of course not.

Don't Tease Me

No one robs a mafia boss if they want to live. The blood drains from my face.

He must notice because he wraps an arm around my waist and pulls me against the hard planes of his body. My hands come to his chiseled chest. "Hey," he says softly. "That wasn't a threat. I know you wouldn't steal from me."

My pulse quickens at his nearness. The simultaneous danger and reassurance of this man who feels so much larger-than-life than any guy I've dated before. "How do you know?" I persist.

"I know people. You have moral standards."

"What else do you think you know about me?"

"I know the fact that you need this place is the only reason you're getting involved with a guy like me. I know it goes against your better instincts. But I also know you liked the sex, and you're ready for more."

I stare at him, shocked at how easily he reads me. My nipples go hard at the mention of sex—he's right on all accounts. I do want him again. I liked the sheer animalism of the way he handled me. The confidence. The dominant but attentive way he touched my body. And how he was in tune with me. Licking my lips, I ask, "So, what do I need to know about, um, our arrangement?"

"Here's the deal. You make yourself available to me. If you're not working at the hair salon, your time is mine. You don't have to sit around and wait for me—I'll text you in advance, but you don't tell me you're busy, yeah? If you have plans, you change them."

"Okay."

"No men here, ever. You don't sleep with or date other men."

"*Capisce*," I say, trying out my Italian.

His lips twitch. "*Capito*," he corrects.

"*Capito.* Sorry. I'm a quick learner, I promise."

"Yeah, you're a smart girl, I know that. You listen more than you talk, and you don't make dumb remarks."

"Is that your definition of smart?"

He looks amused, his brown eyes all-knowing, the thick dark lashes giving him a permanently sultry look. "Yeah."

A lick of heat sets my nether region on fire when our eyes catch and hold.

"This is an arrangement. I'm not your boyfriend. Don't make demands of me. I'll take good care of you, but I call the shots."

"Understood," I agree. I chew on the inside of my cheek. "You're definitely not married?"

He shakes his head, and I'm relieved to see there's no hesitation. "Definitely not married. No girlfriend, either. I'm a one-woman guy. I won't fuck around on you. I just like things clearly defined."

"I have to admire a man who knows what he wants."

Bobby winks. Damn. He's so hot. I seriously don't see why someone hasn't locked him down yet. Maybe because he won't let it happen.

"One more rule. The most important one." He holds my gaze with an intensity that makes my belly flip. "You don't talk about me to anyone. You don't tell your friends or anyone else when I come or when I go. Not what I say. Not what we do. Not anything. Understand?"

I swallow. He said he's not a thug, but whatever he does definitely isn't legal. "Yes."

"Breaking any of my rules will get you punished."

Um...*punished?* My ass clenches at the threat. I draw in a breath, hardly daring to ask. "Punished, how?"

One corner of his mouth lifts, and I catch a wicked gleam in his eye. "Spanked. Whipped. Tied up and fucked hard. Put on your knees and gagged with my cock." He raises a brow. "Do you consent to that?"

My nipples get hard. I let out a nervous laugh. I expected him to say *whacked*. Maybe I've watched too many old *Sopranos* episodes. But Bobby Manghini has a kinky side, it seems. No wonder he prefers an *arrangement*–calling the shots is part of his kink. The idea of his asserting his authority over me with physical punishment doesn't dim his appeal. Not one bit.

"Yes," I say.

His lips curve, and his gaze is warm on me. "Do we have a deal?"

I nod. "Deal."

In a flash, he pulls my blouse up over my head and backs me against a barstool. He moves in for a kiss at the same time his fingers work the buttons on my designer jeans. He attacks my lips with his–tongue demanding entry as he kisses and sucks.

Heat suffuses my body. I stand on my tiptoes, one arm around his neck, trying to keep up with the onslaught. He has my jeans down in record time, giving me no chance to feel shy about stripping in front of the giant glass window overlooking the city lights.

"Lexi, you're so hot," he murmurs, straightening and cupping one breast while his other hand holds my nape.

Hearing my name and his appreciation makes my pussy clench with excitement. He slides his hand inside my bra and rubs my nipple between his thumb and forefinger. I arch into him, breathless.

Settling his hands on my hips, he murmurs, "jump". When I do, he picks me up and sits me on the countertop, where he spreads my knees and pulls my panties to the side. I jerk when his tongue meets my pussy, the shock of sensation making me throw my head back and moan. I fall back onto my forearms, closing my eyes and squirming under his ministrations.

I love having my pussy licked, but it never makes me come. Bobby twists two fingers inside me, stroking my inner wall, then pumping, but I still can't crest the peak. In general, I have a hard time orgasming with a partner, which is why I questioned his cockiness last night.

He pulls me down from the counter and leads me to the sofa, where he bends me over the padded arm. After sliding my panties down to my thighs, he shocks me with a sharp slap on my ass. I gasp and try to stand, but he holds me down with a hand at my low back, continuing to spank my bare ass with the flat of his hand. The slaps sound loud, and the initial impact makes me jerk, but the sting doesn't set in for a few moments. When it does, I begin to buck, trying to convey I've had enough. I've never been spanked before—during sex or otherwise—and damn, it's a little intense!

He gives me four more hard swats then grips the cheek of my ass and squeezes. "Mmm...this is delicious."

I moan, the fire not just on the surface of my ass but burning inside me. I want him–want completion–with a desperation I've never before felt.

"Please..." I plead. My heart thuds with the excitement of it all–sex with a near stranger, the proposed sugar daddy arrangement, and the dominant way Bobby handles me.

I hear the crinkle of a wrapper and the snap of a condom. He pushes into me easily–I must be wetter than the ocean right now.

Drunk with need, my eyelids flutter as he holds my hips and pounds into me. When he twists both my arms behind my back as if restraining me—as if taking me by force rather than invitation—I shatter, bucking. My muscles contract around his cock in endless waves until he makes a guttural sound and slams into me, shooting his load.

Dazed, I collapse in a boneless mass, my face buried in the soft cushions. I hardly notice Bobby pull out or move until he pulls me up and turns me around, scooping under my knees and shoulders to carry me to a large, beautifully appointed bedroom.

I wrap my arms around his neck and mumble, "Okay, you were right about the sex."

He chuckles, a warm rumbling in his chest. "I'm always right. Even if I'm wrong." He winks.

I laugh. "You're the boss."

"Good girl." He lays me down on the bed. The two words wrap around me like a blanket, swaddling in the pleasure. I'm a pleaser by nature, and Bobby's not hard to please. I don't have to guess at what he wants, don't have to try to perform. He takes care of everything–tells me clearly what he wants from me and what to do, taking charge of my body. Moving me, positioning me, restraining me, spanking me. Praising me when I accept it all. Who knew pleasure is a boss to surrender to.

I roll to my back and blink up at him, admiring the sleek lines of his muscular torso, imagining what he looks like naked. Before tonight, I had no idea I would react to a spanking or being handled roughly, but that was the fastest I've ever come to orgasm in my life. So effortless. Did he see something in me I missed my entire adult life?

"So...about that. I know people get spanky during sex and all, but what made you think I would like it?"

He crawls over me, smirking. "I didn't. It's just what *I* wanted to do."

* * *

Bobby

I watch Lexi flush as she digests my words, probably half-offended, half-turned on. I could have described all the little signs she gave that told me she's the type who got turned on by dominance, but revealing my hand would only dim the electricity between us.

I kiss her, my palm roaming over her soft skin. I never feel tender until *after* sex, the actual act always bringing out my full aggression and desire to control. Finding a girl like Lexi, who doesn't just tolerate my quirk but responds with a matching level of desire, is more than a win–it's a fucking goldmine. I want things to work out with her.

I trace her cheekbone with my thumb. "So, can you handle being my girl?"

She moves to sit up, but I hold her down, rolling on top and pinning her hands over her head. She smiles up at me like the move warms her. Like I'm planting butterfly kisses across her skin, not restraining her. She's definitely a submissive. My kind of girl.

"I think so," she murmurs. Her blue-eyed gaze turned sultry, but I sense the tinge of nervous energy behind it. I don't mind—it proves her intelligence. She's walking into the arrangement with open eyes.

I land another kiss on her mouth. "I'll take good care of you, sweetheart," I murmur and mean it. I like to pamper my women. Flowers, dinner, chocolate. I'll treat her right.

Releasing her wrists, I roll off her and climb out of the bed. "I hate to leave, but I gotta get home," I say.

My twin nineteen-year-old daughters have lived with me since they started college this fall, and I like to be around enough to know what they're up to. I agreed to give them some independence if they stayed with me, rather than stay at home with their mom in the suburbs or move into the dorms at NYU last fall. Yeah, I'm protective as hell, and the idea of them living in the city, in a stinking dorm, made me crazy. I attempt to provide a stable landing pad in hopes they'll keep good heads on their shoulders.

I also don't want Lexi to think I'm her boyfriend. I'm not the guy who holds her at night and makes her coffee in the morning. Not unless we're on vacation together. This is transactional–that's the way I like it.

"I'm sorry there isn't much to eat in the kitchen, but here's some cash, so you can go out for a nice breakfast on me." I drop two hundred dollar bills on the dresser. "Are you cutting hair tomorrow?"

She nods. "Eleven to six."

"Text me the name and address of your salon, and I'll pick you up after work." I lean over and give her a kiss.

"Thank you."

I drop another hundred on the dresser. "You probably don't have any clothes to wear, do you? If you have time, go buy yourself a short skirt, I want to see those long legs on full display."

She grins. "As you wish, my lord."

I lean over and smack her ass again, hard enough to make her yelp. "You'd better watch out, little girl, or I'll give you a real taste of authority."

I love watching her eyes dilate in response to my threat. I give her another kiss and leave, the victory of my new conquest putting a spring into my step.

Lexi is one hundred times better than my last few mistakes. She might even be a keeper.

Not that I even know what that means. I certainly don't want to be in a romantic relationship with someone. I don't need the hassle of a girlfriend, and I definitely never plan to marry again.

So I guess Lexi is a keeper in terms of a longer arrangement.

Even as I think it, the smarter part of me acknowledges that's not a thing. A girl like Lexi isn't going to stick around long-term without me having to offer more than I'm willing to give.

But I don't have to worry about that now.

For now, we've come to an agreement that suits us both.

If this doesn't work for her in the future, we can renegotiate then.

Chapter Five

Lexi

I get a text from Bobby the next afternoon while I'm at Stylz. *I paid off your landlord, and I'll have your things back to you by tonight. I'll meet you at the apartment instead of at work.*

I text back my thanks with heart, kiss, and high heel shoe emojis, affirming my gratitude will be shown in the way he expected.

Oddly, I don't feel as cheap and dirty in the light of day as I thought I would. I feel lighthearted. Yes, I'm essentially a paid call girl. Not something to write home about. Obviously not a long-term arrangement. But I feel more supported than I can ever remember. Yeah, I'm in bed with a mobster, which is probably dangerous as fuck, but for the moment, the perks outweigh the risk. I really didn't want to sleep on Gina's couch or move back home with my mom. That would feel like defeat. Yeah, this is way better. For now.

As I let these new perceptions land in me, I own that last night I felt sexy, desirable, and cared for. Waking up in the luxurious apartment this morning was amazing. It's funny how much clearer your thoughts are when you're in beautiful surroundings. My world completely pivoted with a yes to Bobby–to this agreement–that feels like a yes to me, to being treated for a change. I'm so ready for something going my way. And so far, the strings attached aren't so distasteful. The sex rocked my world.

I go shopping after work to buy some clothes, picking out a short skirt as Bobby requested. When I return to the apartment, I find two beefy and tattooed guys moving boxes from a truck into the elevator.

I spy my cosmetic bag on the top of one of the open boxes. "Oh! That's mine?"

"Are you Lexi?" one of them asks.

"Yes!"

"Great. Bobby sent us. I'm Tommy. This is Junior. We've got all your stuff."

I gape in surprise, trying to peek in the boxes they're moving. "Did you pack it, too?"

"Yep," the young man called Junior said. "Bobby has storage in the basement of this place. That's where we moved your furniture."

Oh God. The thought of them moving my flea market-finds embarrasses the hell out of me. At least Bobby didn't see them.

I follow them into the apartment. "Thank you so much. This was really nice of you."

"Hey, anything for Bobby's girl," Tommy says.

Bobby's girl. I don't mind the sound of that. Especially considering the perks that seem to come with it. And Tommy sounded like he respects me because I'm Bobby's girl. No questions asked. Just acceptance.

I search through the boxes, digging out my sexiest

lingerie and a bustier to wear with the requested skirt for our date. Bobby did his part. I'm definitely going to do mine. I notice I'm having fun. There's a lightheartedness, a playfulness, I haven't felt since before the accident.

When I hear his key scrape in the lock, I rub my glossed lips together and trot out to meet him. "Hey."

He looks as sexy as ever, his designer suit draping his muscular frame with a slouchy elegance.

I did my best to impress, and my appearance has its intended effect. He closes the door and leans his back against it. "Oh no." His eyes rake up and down my body.

My breath hitches. "What?"

"I cannot go out with you looking like that."

I cock my head, assuming he's pleased, but not sure. I don't know him well enough yet. "Why not?"

"Because I will be blue-balling it all through dinner."

I smile seductively. "Well, maybe we should take care of that before we go, then."

"Nah," he says, not moving from the door. "I don't want to muss your hair when you're looking so good."

"Muss my hair?" I smirk, grabbing the hem of my short skirt and yanking it up to flash him my see-through mesh and lace panties before I kick off my heels and go running for the bedroom. *Catch me if you can.*

The sound of his low chuckle precedes thundering footsteps, and he catches me around the waist just as I reach the door. I give a shriek of excitement.

"Now you're in big trouble." He sets my feet back on the ground. I start to take off again, only to have him block me and pin me back against the wall by my upper arms.

I kick my dangling feet, giggling. He insinuates his thigh between mine, leaning forward and dragging his mouth up my neck. I pant, wrapping my legs around his waist.

"Oh God," he moans. "Do you know what you're doing to me? You're going to get yourself fucked right here against this wall. Is that what you want?"

His words set me on fire, the coarseness of his language flicking the switch from hot to flaming. His fingers bite into the flesh of my arms, but I don't want it to end. "Yeah," I breathe.

His eyelids flicker, and he inhales deeply, releasing my arms to cup my breasts. With my back planted against the wall and my legs wound around his waist, he holds me pinned in position. I lose my mind completely, so crazed with desire I can't wait another instant to have him inside me. I reach for the button on his slacks, managing to undo it as he kneads my ass with his hands. He reaches back with one hand to grab his wallet out of his pocket before he wriggles to shimmy his slacks down. After retrieving a condom from the billfold and putting it between his teeth, he tosses the wallet on the floor with the pants. He slips his finger in the gusset of my panties. Finding me wet, he makes an approving noise. I snatch the condom from his mouth and rip open the wrapper, grasping his cock with a firm grip to slide it on.

Bobby shifts his position against me and yanks my panties to the side to push the head of his sheathed cock against my entrance. I gasp as he shoves deeper, filling me. He holds my thighs and uses the wall to brace me as he pumps in and out, the sound of our bodies banging the drywall covering the noise of my cries. I nearly sob with need. Bobby's aggression, the way he manhandles me, makes me feel more desirable than I ever felt in my life. As if he finds me so sexy he can hardly control himself, can't make it the extra five feet to the bed, needs me as badly as I now need him.

"Oh God, oh yeah!" he shouts, coming.

I spasm around his cock, his orgasm the only excuse I need to come. I clutch his shoulders, digging my nails into his arms as my vision turns black with sparks of light.

"Bobby," I pant, sounding hoarse. So far he's three for three. So much for trouble getting off with a partner. With Bobby Manghini, it doesn't seem to be an issue.

He remains pressed inside me, breathing against my neck, fingers gripping the flesh of my thighs.

"I'm pretty sure that messed up your hair," he says when his breath slows.

I give a contented sigh, and he releases me, easing out as he gently lowers my legs.

"That was a very nice start to our date." He pulls up his pants and zips them.

I lower my skirt and straighten the bustier. "Yes," I agree.

"I will have to make sure to reward you properly."

I have no idea what he means, but his words excite me, making me eager to win his approval during every encounter.

We freshen up and head out. He drives me to L'amore, a fancy Italian restaurant where the maitre d' greets him by name.

"Sal, this is my girl, Lexi."

The maitre d' actually bows to me. "A pleasure to meet you."

"If she comes here, with or without me, you take good care of her and put it on my tab, *capisce*?"

"Absolutely, Mr. Manghini."

Um wow. I try to hide my pleasure at the idea of having free rein to dine on his dime. I have seriously been living on canned tuna and frozen burritos. This is a massive treat for me.

The waiter comes and Bobby looks over the top of the wine menu at me. "Do you prefer wine or a cocktail?"

"You decide." I'm honestly a little overwhelmed by all the new luxuries coming at me at once.

Bobby seems to like that answer because his gaze turns warm. He orders a bottle of Shiraz. "And Anthony?" he calls our waiter back.

"Yes, Mr. Manghini?"

"This is Lexi, my girl. I want you to treat her like a princess, understand? If she says 'jump', you ask 'how high?' Got it?"

"Of course, Mr. Manghini." Anthony gives me a deferential bow of his head. "Don't hesitate to ask me for anything."

Okay, now I really feel like a princess. No one has ever said anything like that for or about me before. I work a service-type job. I make the clients feel like queens, not the other way around. I'm the one fluffing people up–I don't get fluffed. It's almost too much, like I want to tell the waiter he doesn't have to–that I'm a peasant too, and he shouldn't worry about me. But screw that. I created this situation out of nothing. Two nights ago, I was literally almost on the street. I'm not going to refuse abundance when it knocks on my door–even if it's only temporary. Or perhaps, *especially* because it's only temporary. I'm going to milk the hell out of this situation with Bobby while I'm in it.

The waiter leaves, and Bobby's gaze dips to my breasts, and I realize my nipples are standing on end, pointing out my thrill to him, even through my strapless bra. "If you are trying to impress me, it worked," I confide.

Bobby grins. "Glad to hear it, *bambina*. You take care of

me, and I'll take care of you, Lex. Speaking of which." He reaches into his pocket. "I have a present for you."

He hands me a new iPhone, the latest model.

I stare at it, slightly confused. I mean, I'm happy to receive any gift, but it's not like I needed a new phone. I would've rather had the cash for it to pay off Arissa for my rent at Stylz.

"It's untrackable and untappable," he says.

Ah. Now I understand.

"Gimme your old phone, and I'll put the sim card in."

I hand over my phone, and he makes the swap.

"Use the calendar app for your hair appointments. It's shared with me, so I can see what time you have to go in and get off."

I blink. Wow. Is that a red flag? What am I getting myself into?

"Yes, I do own you, now." His wink softens the words.

I flush. There's only one way to play this, and that's to go with the flow. See his control issues as a kink, not a personality flaw.

"You're the boss," I say.

* * *

Bobby

After another sizzling round between the sheets with Lexi, I drive home and park in the garage, glad to see both my daughters' cars in the driveway. I have to exercise an enormous amount of restraint not to still treat them as if they're in high school. Lord knows, I want to give them a midnight curfew and demand a full accounting of where and with whom they've been. Then personally visit every guy who takes an interest in them and threaten to cut off his hands if he tries anything with my baby girls.

"Hi, Daddy!" Juliana calls from the kitchen. "I'm making meatballs!"

"At midnight?" I give her a peck on the cheek and sit down on a barstool at the breakfast counter.

"Yeah, why not?" she says.

"Well, when are you going to eat it, tonight?"

She shrugs. "I don't know. Maybe. It will just be ready for whenever we want to eat it."

I smile. "Thanks, sweetie. I like it when you cook."

"A fancy invite came for Mario and Sandra's wedding." Juliana points to the opened invitation on the counter.

"Oh yeah, when is it?"

"End of the month."

"Did you put it on the family calendar?"

"Of course. So, where have you been?"

"Yeah, where have you been?" Janine joins us in the kitchen.

"I had a date."

"I knew it! I told you." Juliana looks past me at her sister. "You have a new girlfriend, don't you?"

Smart girls.

"What makes you think so?"

"You got home late last night, and this morning you seemed way too happy. And then you said you weren't going to be around for dinner. So I knew it!"

"Reasonable deduction."

"What's her name?"

I hesitate. I don't like my kinky sex life to collide with real life. With family with a lowercase or Family with a capital F. But for some reason, something about Lexi makes me feel like sharing. Maybe I'm just riding the high of my two orgasms in one night. Maybe I'm just drunk on feeling powerful. Because that's how Lexi makes me feel when I have those blue eyes trained on me. When she says softly, *you're the boss.*

So I tell them more than I should. "Lexi. She's a hair-stylist—she's a knockout and smart, too."

"Are you going to bring her by?"

"Nope."

"Why not?"

"Because you two do not need to be exposed to my dating life."

"Why not?" both girls demand at the same time.

"This is the way it's always been. Why the sudden interest in my love life?"

Janine shrugs. "We just want you to be happy."

"Yeah, Dad," Juliana says. "We've been talking about it. Remember when you and Mom first got divorced, and we said we never wanted you to remarry?"

I nod.

"Well, we're sorry for that. Kids are selfish, you know? We were talking about it, and we feel bad. Now that we're grown up, we obviously see things differently."

I blink at the sudden burning in my eyes. "Thanks, but I like the way things are," I say gruffly.

My phone rings, and seeing Joey's name, I answer it.

"Hey Bobby," Joey says in the clipped tone that means we're going to discuss business. I stand and walk out of the room, away from my daughters' ears, though they know better than to listen in on business conversations.

"What's up?"

"My insider with the FBI said they're sniffing into Manghini Construction. It sounds like it's being driven by democrats who are trying to get the mayor out of office.

They're looking for any payments or kickbacks you made to him for the city construction deals. Will they find anything?"

"I don't know. I don't think so. I made three legitimate campaign contributions—one through each business entity."

"Anything else?"

"Some cash. Fifty grand, maybe, not much. Just a little thank you bonus when we got the contract."

"Well, we can hope he was smart enough not to deposit it in a bank. You should be fine. The worst that could happen is they link the contributions to you and make a big smear campaign out of it. But that's more a problem for the mayor than you, and it's nothing for the Feds to chew on."

"Thanks for the heads' up."

"No problem. I'll keep you posted if I hear anything else."

I end the call and sigh. Feds. They always came sniffing.

Chapter Six

Lexi

My first client isn't until noon, so I spend the morning taking advantage of the building's amenities. The gym is simple but clean and high-quality. I'm not a gym rat, but it's fun to play, so I do a few rounds on the machines. Then I head up to the rooftop pool, which is amazing. I had both to myself.

When I go into Stylz, I'm a new woman.

Until Arissa corners me in the kitchenette. "Listen, Lexi. I know you've had a rough time with the accident and being out of work–"

"No, I know," I cut in. "I owe you a lot. But I can make a payment right now, and I'll give you everything I make today. I just need another month or two to get the back rent paid down, but I promise I'm good for it."

I have the money I'd planned on giving the landlord, plus a couple hundred dollars from Bobby, and now that I don't have to worry about paying rent, I can use all my earnings toward paying her off first, then chipping down my medical bills.

"It's just that you haven't made any payments toward the back pay at all, and—"

"I'm so sorry. It's just taken me a while to climb out of the hole, but I'm starting to catch up." I definitely don't want to explain that I'd prioritized her below my landlord, nor am I going to tell her I got myself evicted.

Behind her, I see Ondrea wincing for me.

"Let me give you the money I have right now." I push past her, even though she doesn't seem finished with whatever kind of ambush this is. I grab my purse and fish out every dollar I have, counting them up and handing them to Arissa, who followed me over. "This is nine hundred eighty-five," I say.

She's not impressed. In fact, she seems even more offended. "You had this much money in your purse the whole time?" she snaps.

Ugh. "Well, no." Crap. Now she thinks I was holding out on her. I'd better just tell her the truth. "I just scraped this together to bring to you today." Not a complete lie.

She narrows her eyes. "You owe me twenty-five hundred more. I need it by the end of this month or you're out."

I somehow hide my gasp, but my heart starts pounding like there's an ax murderer after me. Ondrea makes a horrified face behind Arissa.

She's kicking me out?

I thought we were on better terms than that. I really did. I was never late before the accident. I thought she knew me.

I blink rapidly, trying to keep the tears back.

She must see them because I can see her resolve wobble. "I'm sorry, it's just that I can barely make the rent here, and you haven't shown any signs of catching up."

"I'm catching up!" I insist, even though it's not really

true. "I'll pull together the rest of the money. I promise." I don't know how, but I will.

"Good."

She walks away, and I get busy, trying to pretend things aren't completely awkward for me here now.

Even if I figure out how to put together that much money by the end of the month, I'm honestly not sure I want to stay here now. I love Ondrea and a few of the other stylists here, but...ugh.

I have no right to resent her for leaning on me, either. Of course, she has a business to run. I guess I'm just...hurt, honestly. We were friendly before.

Now it feels icky.

God, I hope I get the trainer job.

* * *

Bobby

"Mayor Randolph. What can I do for you?"

"Cut the crap, Manghini. You know damn well why I'm calling. I had phone calls from five reporters asking about my contracts with you. What the fuck is going on?"

Reporters. Fuck.

How did that happen? Someone at the FBI must've leaked the investigation. Talk about an organization in crisis.

"I'll call you back."

"The fuck you w–"

Fanculo. I end the call and drop my phone to the floor, crushing it with my heel. I open the bottom drawer of my desk and pull out a burner phone, still in its plastic container. As I tear it open, I stride out of my office and into the hallway, taking the the stairs down at a fast pace.

Once I'm on the street, I call the mayor back on his cell phone.

"What were you thinking calling me from your office line? Stop acting so fucking guilty–you're putting an noose around your own neck."

The mayor goes silent. "Was that a threat?"

"Jesus," I mutter. "Do you need one? Aren't you worried enough about your own neck to smarten up?"

I hear him exhale.

"This is likely being stirred up by democrats anxious to take your seat. Don't give them a reason to. What did you do with the cash I gave you?"

"I've been spending it. But what's left is in a safe in my home."

"Move it. Clean your house and office of anything incriminating in case they pull a warrant. I'll do the same. Meet me tonight at the Starbucks on 5th and Appleton, and we'll go over the bids you received to discuss why mine was superior, then you'll have the answer for the press."

"You seem pretty sure of yourself."

"I am sure. You've got nothing to worry about, except your own erratic behavior. Smarten up. You're the goddamn mayor. Act like one."

"Fuck you, Manghini."

"See you tonight." I end the call before he can curse at me again.

Goddammit. I don't like any of this business.

I generally keep my ducks in order, but it's time to make sure they are military-fucking-straight.

Chapter Seven

Lexi

I plop onto a barstool at Swank and wait for Gina to come over. She's working behind the bar tonight as a bartender, which is new for her. I think she's still in training for it.

It's been four days since I've heard from Bobby.

I guess I should be glad. I have a sugar daddy who's given me the use of a beautiful luxury apartment and doesn't make a huge demand on my time.

That's what I keep telling myself.

But that's not at all how I feel.

I feel like my new crush is blowing me off.

That's the dumb part. Bobby made it clear he wasn't a boyfriend and not to have those kinds of expectations of him. He also told me he was a busy man. So this whole situation was laid out clearly for me. I have absolutely no reason to be angry. Or right to miss him.

But I do miss him.

I also have been debating whether or not to ask him for a loan to pay off Arissa, but I haven't decided on whether I wanted to hassle him when he's already paid off my landlord and given me cash this month. I guess I was thinking I'd play it by ear when I saw him, but I haven't seen him.

"Well?" she prompts when she arrives. "How's it working out with your sugar daddy?"

I smile. "Yeah, it's the real deal. He's great."

Gina beams. "I thought you guys would be a good fit! How is the sex?"

"Honestly? Amazing. I'm supposed to be at his beck and call, but I haven't heard from him in four days, and I can't stop thinking about him. I'm almost ready to call him!"

"Oh my God." Gina affects a scandalized tone.

"Well, I'm not falling for him or anything," I say, probably a little too quickly. "Is that what you think?"

Gina holds up her palms. "Hey, I didn't say anything. I've just never heard you talk this way about a guy before."

"Well, you were right. He's hot."

"Like what? What's so hot? What's he do?"

My face heats remembering how he bent me over the sofa and spanked me. Screwed me hard against a wall. Fingerfucked me on the kitchen counter. "He's rough. Totally demanding. But in tune. Does that make sense?"

Her brow furrows. "Like what?"

"I mean, he knows when I start getting nervous and slows down, but if I'm on board, he's the type to throw you up against the wall and fuck your brains out."

Gina raised her eyebrows. "Did he do that?"

I do the slow, awed, satisfied nod.

"Wow."

"Yeah. Wow. Total wow."

"So, what's the scoop? How often do you see him? When do you see him next?"

Butterflies stir in my belly. I haven't heard from him in four days, even though I texted a couple times. I hope my eviction drama didn't turn him off. I definitely need to see him because Arissa, the owner at the salon told me I have to pay in full by the end of the month, or she'll find a new renter for my chair. I will give her everything I make, but it isn't enough. I hoped to see Bobby a couple times to supplement the income enough to at least pay one month's rent and get Arissa off my back.

Before I can answer a skinny blonde waltzes up and takes the barstool next to me. Gina shoots me a meaningful look, which I don't know how to interpret.

"What can I get you?" Gina slides a cocktail napkin in front of the blonde.

"Cosmo. Were you talking about Bobby?"

I whip my head around to look at the woman.

She shrugs. "I saw you leaving here with him last weekend. Is that who you're talking about?"

Gina clamps her mouth shut and gets busy making the drink.

Aw, fuck. This must be the ex-girlfriend. Or ex-sugar baby. Or whatever. Well, hell.

I'm not jealous since she's the ex, but I still don't like her.

Although... I guess I could use some more information about the guy. Like knowing what this chick did wrong to lose him. That might be helpful. Because I really need this situation to last long enough for me to get back on my feet. I'll need enough money for a deposit on my own place, and hopefully a small cushion of savings.

"Yeah. Did you used to date him?"

The blonde nods. "I still do, sometimes," she says, and my eyes narrow. "I'm Stacy. Did he mention me?"

Gina shakes her head when the blonde isn't looking, rolling her eyes.

"Um, no."

"How about you? Have you seen him since that night?"

"Yes. I moved into his apartment." I'm not usually alpha female, but I guess I'm feeling a little territorial right now. She's obviously still interested in Bobby, and it pisses me off.

The blonde's lips tighten. Gina sets the drink in front of her, and Stacy drains the glass. "I'll have another, please." Turning to me, she produces a saccharine smile. "I lived in that apartment for two months," she boasts. "But, things just didn't work out between us. He's too controlling. He gets off on being the one in charge, you know?"

Obviously. That's his kink, bimbo. I make a non-committal sound.

"Listen, do you have his new number? Because I tried to call him this week, but it sounds like he swapped phones out again. He does that a lot, you know."

I don't want to bite. I really don't. But I haven't heard from the guy either. "What do you mean?"

Stacy shrugs. "Something about keeping lines secure. I have no idea. But every so often, he dumps his number and starts over with a new phone."

"Oh. Well how are you supposed to get a hold of him then?" Maybe that's why he hasn't returned my texts.

"Oh, you don't have his new number, either?" Stacy flashes that nasty smile again.

Grr.

She opens her phone. "I could give you his home number."

I narrow my eyes. "Why don't you just call his home number, then?"

"Well, I have, but he hasn't picked up."

I don't trust Stacy even the slightest bit, but her story about the phones might be true. I take out my own phone and scroll through the contacts to Bobby's name. "Yeah, I will take that home number, if you don't mind," I say.

"No problem." Stacy hands me her phone.

I take it and copy the numbers into my contacts, trying to figure out if I dare call him there. He said he wasn't my boyfriend. Calling his home line probably comes off as needy.

A cold sensation slithers through me. What if, despite everything he said, he *is* married? I mean, why else would he keep his girlfriend at a separate apartment where he never sleeps?

I'm tempted to call the number just to see if a woman answers.

"May I see the number you have for him?" Stacy asks when I finish.

Well, crap. I totally set myself up for that, didn't I. Somehow, I feel certain Bobby won't like me handing out his number. I mean, what did he tell me? Not to talk about him to anyone.

Fuck.

"Uh...sure." I am so bad at saying no. It's really a skill I need to develop.

I show her the number, and the other woman shakes her head. "No, that's the same one I have. It's no good. Thanks, anyway."

Thank God. I really didn't want to piss Bobby off.

Stacy slips off the barstool and takes her second drink with her.

Gina leans her forearms on the bar. "That was weird."

"I know. I kept waiting for her head to spin around and

fire to come out of her mouth or something. You don't really think she was being helpful, do you?"

Gina shakes her head. "No. She wants him back and is trying to keep her enemies close. I'd watch out for that one if I were you."

"I will."

I take the bus home and sit on the sofa considering. Why hasn't Bobby called? Is this a normal time span between dates for him? I almost wish I asked Stacy. But that would mean revealing that I'm being blown off.

If he does have a new phone, why hasn't he given me the new number? Could he have lost my number?

I consider calling his house. If a woman answers, I know he's a lying piece of shit. If he answers, I can just let him know I miss him.

I pick up the phone and dial, my heart rate increasing as I wait for someone to pick up.

* * *

Bobby

After an eleven-hour day at the office followed by a meeting with the don about the possible FBI raid, I finally make it home. The house phone rings, and I pick up.

"Hello?"

"Um, hi!"

I recognize Lexi's voice.

I blow out my breath, short on patience and high on suspicion right now. "Why are you calling me here?" I demand. I don't even know how she got the number. "I'll call you right back." I hang up and call back with my new cell phone.

"What the hell, Lexi? Landlines are almost always

tapped. Now the Feds have your number, you know. Did you want to be on their watch list?"

"Oh God. I'm sorry." She sounds nervous. "I just—"

I interrupt. "Why didn't you call my cell? I texted you the new number."

"No you didn't!" she protests.

Now I'm fully annoyed because I definitely did. Then another realization hits home. *"Where did you get my home number?"*

She doesn't answer.

Fanculo. The last thing I need right now is female drama. Another psycho girl like Stacy hounding me at the same time I have the feds breathing down my neck.

I need to see her face to get to the root of this. "Are you at the apartment?"

"Um, yes, uh huh." Her voice is overly-agreeable.

"I'll be right over."

I drive to my apartment building, trying to decipher her behavior. She says she didn't receive my text with my new number. But how and why did she dig out my home number? And the fact that she went to the trouble bothers me.

A lot.

There's a reason I don't want a girlfriend. I want things on my own terms–not on hers. This feels intrusive and needy.

Definitely reeks of Stacy-behavior, which I thought Lexi was above.

I find her on the couch watching the television when I come in, but she immediately turns it off and stands to walk toward me. She definitely looks sorry, which, I have to admit, is a cute look on her. Some of my irritation starts to seep away.

She's not nuts. She's not acting defensive or playing dumb.

This was a misunderstanding. One we can definitely work out with a talk and some sexy punishment.

My dick stirs in my pants at the prospect.

"You're in trouble with me, Lexi," I warn.

* * *

Lexi

Crap. I should not have pissed off the mob boss. Made man. Whatever he is. I don't want this arrangement to end. I mean, I *really* don't want it to end. Not just from a financial standpoint—and my money situation is still dire. But I also hate the idea that I've irritated Bobby. Because I really like him.

"I know." I try to appear calm. "I'm sorry, Bobby."

I've been pacing the apartment, attempting to not freak out.

"I checked my text messages after we hung up, and I found your text from a few days ago. It didn't show up as a new message for some reason, so I hadn't noticed it. I'm really sorry."

Regardless of having his new number or not, I shouldn't have called him at home. Now he's mad, and I'm not even sure what that means with a guy like him. Will he break up with me? Kick me out of the apartment? Punish me? He threatened punishment if I broke his rules, will that be the worst of it? Or was that just kinky talk?

I fight tears now as I realize I'm in way over my head. Why I thought getting mixed up with a mobster was a good idea is beyond me.

The grim look on Bobby's face when he came in has

already softened. He takes in my tears and sighs. "Come here, doll." He holds his arms out.

Holy yes. I suck in a breath and close the distance between us. He folds me into his arms in an embrace. I melt into him, allowing his strength to envelope me.

"I'm sorry," I say into his suit jacket.

"It'll be okay." He kisses the top of my head. He holds me for a moment, then says, "Look at me, baby." When I lift my face, he lowers his head to catch and hold my gaze. "We have rules. The rules are for your safety and mine."

I nod.

"What were you thinking calling my house?"

I swallow, not sure how to answer.

His eyes narrow. "And where did you get my home number, anyway?"

I start to look away, and he catches my chin, gently holding my face in place, my gaze trapped in his. He raises his brows, waiting.

The knot in my belly tightens.

"Lex?"

"I saw your ex-girlfriend at Swank. Stacy? She asked me for your new number."

"Cristo." His jaw clenches. "I see. Did you give it to her?"

"Well, no! I didn't have it. Well, at least I didn't realize I had it. I'm sorry, I never saw your text."

He cocks his head. "So you would have given it to her if you had it?"

Crap. I flush. Somehow I have a feeling he would know if I lied. Instead, I lift my chin. "I wouldn't have needed to because..." I trail off, realizing my argument lacks logic.

"Because?"

I blink back the water brimming in my eyes. "She told

me you switched cell numbers a lot, and I should just call your house. She gave me the number. Then I felt like I had to reciprocate and show her the number I had."

"I see."

"I'm sorry, Bobby. I really fucked up."

His expression softens. "Yes, you did fuck up." He doesn't sound angry anymore, not the way he did on the phone. "Listen, baby, I'm in a dangerous business. I'm keeping you out of it. Stacy is going to get herself hurt if she keeps fucking with my business. And not by me. My organization...doesn't take kindly to fuckery. That's why I keep you completely shielded."

I work to swallow. "I'm really sorry."

He tugs me closer and kisses my forehead. "That was a very sweet apology." His voice softens to a deep rumble. "You're cute when you're sorry." I realize his gaze is heated now, his eyes hooded. "I'm going to enjoy punishing you."

My pussy clenches at the same time my belly flips.

I can't decide if I'm more scared or excited. Whether this is just kink or something to really fear. Maybe a mixture of the two.

I take a step backward. He follows, his movements predatory. He's turned on by whatever it is he's about to do, and that revs my engine, too. He can tie me up. Torture me. Whip me with his belt. So long as he enjoys it, I think I'm good. It's weird, but I'd rather have his punishment any day than his rejection. It's been a short time, but I've already entrained myself to want to please him.

"Am *I* going to enjoy it?" My voice warbles a little as I ask.

He chuckles. "That depends. Do you like a little pain with your pleasure?" He unbuttons the cuff on his sleeve and starts rolling it up.

"I-I dont know."

He tips his head toward the bedroom. "Let's find out. Go in the bedroom and take off your clothes."

My nipples stiffen under my shirt. I obey, excited when I see he's right behind me, following me in. He leans in the doorway and watches me undress as he finishes rolling up his sleeves. My hands tremble unbuttoning my jeans and pulling off my fitted top. I turn to face him, and every inch of my skin heats under his gaze.

"All of them?" I whisper-croak.

He nods, his dark gaze gleaming.

I unhook my bra and toss it on the floor, then step out of my panties.

He unbuckles his belt and slides it out of the loops.

Oh boy. I take a step backward, a whimper crooning in my throat.

He grabs both the pillows from the bed and stacks them on top of one another at the side. "Lie over these."

My heart thuds. My feet don't move.

Bobby waits. "Come on, doll. Take your punishment."

I want to be his good girl. I must crave a little degradation and pain because I'm excited as I stumble forward, climbing over the pillows to lie down as he instructed. My heart continues to thud, but I'm definitely wet between my legs.

He trails his fingers lightly across my ass and down the back of my thigh. "Good girl."

There are those two words again. I don't know why they have such an effect on me, but they do. I crave his praise. Want to satisfy him. To please him.

He winds the buckle end of his belt around his fist, and I try to contain my anxiety by biting the bedspread. I hear the sound a split second before I feel the first lick of leather across my ass. The line of fire surprises me with its sting, but it's not nearly as terrible as I feared. I jump as he lays down the next stripe and the following. Again and again, he brings the belt down, burning my bare flesh with each stroke. I wriggle and roll under the continuous onslaught and find myself counting strokes as a way of managing the intensity. After the first ten, it gets easier, the shock wearing away as my entire ass grows hot. After fifteen though, panic returns.

"Please! I'm sorry!" I gasp.

Bobby doesn't answer, just continues snapping the leather across my tender cheeks.

"Bobby! Please! Please?" I reach back and try to cover my ass, but he catches my wrist and bends it behind my back, restraining me.

"It's over when I decide, Lexi."

Something about his words and the way he's pinning me down flips a switch in me, desire flaring alongside the pain. I want him to go on, want more of his leather, the bite of his belt morphing into something almost pleasurable. Almost, but not quite.

I struggle against his hold, my hips undulating more wantonly now. "Please," I beg, though I hardly know what I want. "Please."

He stops and rubs my smarting ass. "Do you call me at home, Lex?" His voice is soft. As soothing as his touch.

"Never," I whimper.

"Do you talk about me with other people? Give out my number?"

"No, Bobby."

"Good girl."

Pleasure flushes through me viscerally.

He releases the wrist he pinned and strokes his hand

down the length of my back to rest on my smarting ass. "You took that so well." He's all praise now, and his praise is definitely my kink.

I moan at his touch, lost in the endorphins from the pain and the flames of need. I part my legs–an offering. Or maybe a request.

He immediately slides two fingers between them, and I moan softly. "You need me to hold you, or are you ready for my cock?" His voice is deep and gravelly, like he got even more turned on by my punishment than I did.

"I'm ready," I murmur.

Chapter Eight

Bobby

I'd be lying if I said I don't have a sadistic streak.

I'm a kinky bastard, and punishing Lexi gets me harder than stone. She surrendered to me like a sweetheart, and I want to be sure she gets her reward now. If she needed to be wrapped in a blanket and fed ice cream, I would've done it. But I'm definitely ready to reward her in other ways if she's down.

I lie down beside her. "Come here, *bambina*."

Lexi looks so beautiful right now. I love seeing her naked, ass reddened by my belt, her hair falling in her face. She can't quite meet my eye, which is cute as hell. I pull her mouth to mine, kissing her plump lips with a bruising ferocity.

She responds in kind, instantly winding her arms around my neck, kissing back as if eager for the connection. She straddles me, unbuttoning my pants. I tweak her nipple, cup and squeeze her breast. She pulls my pants off and crouches over my cock, taking me into her mouth.

I'm already rock hard for her, and the sensation of her hot, wet mouth closing around my length nearly drives me mad. She brings me to a fever pitch, but I stop her before I come. Grabbing a condom from the bedside table, I rip it open and slide it on.

"Climb on me," I order, my voice rough.

She smiles and crawls up to straddle my cock, rubbing the head over her juicy slit a few times before impaling herself on it.

"Oh God, Lexi," I groan. She feels so. Damn. Good.

She rides me, resting her hands on my shoulders, undulating her back and hips to create a rhythm. Her face flushes, her dilated eyes turn glassy. She begins to move faster, fingers digging into my skin.

Picking up the belt that still lays on the bed, I wrap it around her ass, using it to leverage her hips to meet mine, slamming her against me with a slapping force.

She makes a keening cry and arches, throwing her head back and stilling as she shudders in orgasm. I cup her breasts, pinching both nipples as I watch her ecstatic peak.

After a moment, she opens her eyes, appearing apologetic. "Sorry, I didn't mean to go so fast."

I lift her off. "Climb back over those pillows."

She looks alarmed, but obeys without question.

"I'm not going to spank you again," I say, amused. I climb onto my knees behind her and push in. "That is, unless you need me to."

"No, sir," she says in a small voice.

Damn. This girl is definitely a keeper. I love her submission.

I thrust in and out, the heat from her punished ass magnifying the sense of power I got punishing her.

I pull her arm behind her back, pinning her wrist the

way I did when I whipped her and she bucks in a second orgasm. "You like being restrained, baby? Does that make you come hard around my cock like a good girl?"

"Ohmygod," she breathes.

This girl is my perfect match. I suspected restraining her had changed the tone of the spanking for her, added to the euphoria of domination, and this confirmed it. I slam into her until I reach my own ecstatic crest, which rips through my body like a tsunami. "Hell, yeah! Fuck, yes!" I shout as I spend into the condom.

I collapse over her, and we pant together, our breath becoming one. I wrap her in my arms and roll to my side, my cock still inside her. Delivering punishment and pain always turns me on, and it often forms a bond, but the depth of tenderness I feel for Lexi in this moment is new.

"You okay, baby?" I ask.

"Yeah," she says softly.

When my cock slips out, she lets out a little sigh of disappointment, and I roll her over to face me, stroking her hair out of her eyes. "Good girl," I murmur.

She snuggles closer. "Am I?"

"Yes."

"Are you keeping me?"

"Definitely. We're solid. More than solid. You're perfect for me."

Her sapphire eyes study my face.

I'm still trying to figure out why she reached out. Is she getting clingy? If so, I need to shut that down. I'm not doing a relationship here.

The irony of the fact that I just basically bonded her to me emotionally by demanding her submission and rewarding her for it isn't lost on me. I'm a *stronzo*, for sure.

But maybe she reached out for another reason. Maybe

she needed something from me. My protective instincts surge into high gear at that thought.

"Do you need something from me, baby?" I stroke her smooth, soft skin. "Is that why you called me? Do you need money?"

Her eyes fill with tears, which she blinks back. "God," she chokes. "How do you that?"

So I guessed correctly. I shrug. "In my business, you have to have a good read on people."

"I do need money," she whispers, gulping. "That's not why I called, though. I wasn't even going to ask you for it...at least, I hadn't decided whether I should or not."

I wish to fuck I'd asked sooner if she had other troubles. I'd assumed I'd taken care of her immediate problems with the landlord and getting her things back, but clearly she has other stressors.

"No, no, baby," I reassure her. "You belong to me. That means I take care of you. You can call me when you need help. Just not at home."

Lexi starts to tremble in my arms, holding back tears.

"Don't cry, *bambi*. How much do you need? What's going on?"

She ducks her chin, pressing her forehead against my chest as the tears emerge. "I owe rent at the salon. I'm not an employee there, I just rent the chair. I'm way behind on rent, and the owner told me if I don't pay by the end of the month, I'm out. I guess this isn't my week."

"Aw, sweetheart. I wish I'd known." I caress her back, the natural curve sensuous under my palm. "How much?"

"Twenty-five hundred."

Chump change. I should've left that much for her the last time I saw her. I kiss the place where her ear meets her face, then her temple. "I'll take care of it," I murmur.

***

Lexi

Tears of relief squeeze out of the corners of my eyes. "Thank you."

Bobby runs his hand up and down my back. "It's my pleasure. You're my girl. I'll take care of your problem. Besides, I like having you owe me."

I narrow my eyes with mock suspicion. "What exactly will I owe you?"

Bobby grins. "What do you have to offer?"

I laugh. "Not much. A lifetime's worth of free haircuts?"

"Hmm."

"How about anal?"

He laughs, cupping my ass and squeezing it. He draws his finger up my crack, making me squirm as he nears my back hole. "This hot little body already belongs to me. Doesn't it, sweetheart?"

I rub my clit over his thick muscular thigh, his words making me ache. "Yes."

"I might collect on a haircut or two."

I snuggle against him. Am I crazy for feeling so warm toward a man who just took his belt to my ass? Possibly.

"I'm not judging you–at all, baby–but how did you get so far behind financially?"

I sag. "A car t-boned mine last fall. I ended up in the hospital with a concussion and knee surgery. I couldn't work for weeks, and I didn't have health insurance, so the hospital bills cost me thirty grand."

"Ah. That's why you get so nervous in the car?"

I exhale. "Yeah. I couldn't afford to buy a new car, and

so I guess I didn't get back on the horse soon enough because now I can't stand to be in one."

"Sounds like PTSD. I know someone who can help you release that pretty quickly, if you want."

I look up at him, trying to gauge whether he's serious.

He shrugs. "What? I've had shit I had to work through."

I lean up on my elbow and trail my nails through the hair on his chest. "You did?" I want to know more about this man. I know he said the Family business is off-limits as a topic, but I'd take any crumbs about him or his personal life. He's a total mystery to me.

"Yeah." He looks up at the ceiling. He's quiet so long I think that's all he's going to say, but then he says, "My dad was gunned down in front of me when I was sixteen."

I silence my gasp, hold my breath to give him the space to share more.

"I, uh, had to take care of the situation myself."

My heart pounds in my chest, aching for his teenage self, thrown into battle at such a young age. "Do you mean..." I hesitate because I know he gets edgy about questions. I never want him to think I'm an informer or that I would turn on him with information I have.

He nods. "I took care of his killer."

That's what I thought he meant. I hold in the sob that chokes my throat for him.

"So I became a made man at sixteen."

Made man. My mind shuffles through the mafia lore I've learned from television and movies. They become made men after killing someone, I think.

"Yeah, that's traumatic." I try to make my voice sound light, but it catches a little.

Bobby pulls my hand to his lips and kisses my fingers. "I thought I was fine. Became the man of the house, took care of the family. The don put me to work and made me rich. I thought I was a man, so I married young. For years afterward, I was twitchy—if a door banged open, I'd draw my gun, that kind of thing. And then it got worse, I developed this weird thing about blood. Every time I saw it, I went into fight or flight. Not great for a guy in my line of work." His rueful smile twists my heart.

"No." I keep my voice soft.

"I was a dick about it—I didn't want anyone to know. I'm an alpha male—we don't show weakness, you know? And then one day, one of my girls had a bloody nose, and I just... blacked out. My wife—ex-wife now—said I drew a gun. Not on them, but in front of them, like I was trying to protect them from something. Either way, it was dangerous and unforgivable. That's when I finally admitted I needed help."

"Bobby," I whisper, stunned.

He blinks. "I can't believe I just told you that story. There's only one person in the world besides my ex-wife and kids who knows it, and that was the therapist I saw for it."

I try to ignore the trickle of pleasure that gives me. That he shared such a personal story with me. That it's not something he shares with every girl he's had in this apartment. "Thank you. I'm honored," I murmur.

His lips tick up, and he kisses my forehead. "So anyway, the therapy I did was fast and effective. It's not like some lie-on-a-couch-and-whine-shit. It's called EMDR, have you heard of it?"

I shake my head.

"I don't really know how it works, but basically you move your eyes left and right while you tell the story of what happened, and it erases all the automatic physical responses that get triggered by the trauma. It's a nervous system reset."

I find this apparently open-minded side to him unexpected. He certainly doesn't appear to be the soy protein shake and wheatgrass kind of guy.

"For me, it just took one session–that was it. Do you want to see her?"

"She's not another ex-girlfriend of yours, right?" I don't know why I ask it, maybe the mention of his ex. Maybe I'm starting to feel territorial about this guy–which is definitely a problem since he made it clear we're not dating.

"Nope. Not an ex-girlfriend. And I'm sorry about Stacy. She's having a hard time letting go. If her crazy continues and catches the notice of the organization, I'm gonna have a hard time protecting her."

I shiver at the reminder of the reality of what Bobby is. Despite how safe and protected he makes me feel, his family is very dangerous.

He smiles. "I'm glad you don't seem threatened."

"Ah...I might have wanted to throat-punch her in the moment," I admit. "But I know I have no claim on you. You're not my boyfriend." I try to sound nonchalant, like I really don't give a flying F about the fact that he's not and never will be boyfriend material. Like it doesn't taste like ash on my tongue saying the words.

I need to remember Bobby Manghini isn't a man I can get attached to, despite the way he seems to be worming his way into my heart.

"So...I asked you a question. Wanna try?"

I wriggle closer. "How much does it cost?"

"I'll take care of it. You think I'd suggest it and not pay?"

I smile. "Okay, yeah. I'd like to try it."

"Good girl." He drops another kiss on my forehead.

Ahh, those magic words. The ones that always turn me to mush. It's crazy that being "owned" by Bobby Manghini holds so much appeal, especially considering what he just did to me. But right now it doesn't matter. I feel safe and warm in his strong arms, my problems all handled by him with ease.

"I need to get back home, angel." He sounds regretful. "Are you okay?" He strokes my cheek.

"Well, my ass is on fire, but yeah." I give a wry smile. "I'm okay. Thanks, Bobby."

He kisses me on the lips and starts to get dressed. Pulling out his wallet, he drops a huge wad of cash on the dresser. "I probably have a grand with me now, and I'll bring you the rest tomorrow. I can meet you down at the salon in the afternoon."

Moisture coats my eyes again. "You don't need to. That will be enough to get her off my back. I have until the end of the month to pay the rest."

"Okay. Call me if it's not."

I climb out of bed and wrap my arms around his neck. "I'm sorry about calling you," I whisper into his neck.

He runs his hand down my back and squeezes my ass. "It's over, baby. We're good." He holds me by the nape and kisses me possessively. "And now that I know you're really my girl," he says, "there's nothing I wouldn't do for you."

Really his girl? What does that mean? I thought he wasn't my boyfriend. I stare, wanting to ask, but he's already turned to go. I listen to the sound of him leaving the apartment as I curl back into the luxurious bed.

Now that I know you're really my girl...

Why am I so happy to hear those words?

Chapter Nine

Bobby

I wake wishing I spent the night with Lexi. I'm horny as hell for her. Remembering how hot she looked last night as she took her punishment has me sprouting a full erection–one I have to go into the shower to take care of.

I meant what I said about doing anything for her. I'm still riding the high of our scene last night. The satisfaction of Lexi's submission. The bond we formed.

I've had submissives before—pain sluts who like it dirty. Or who like it during sex but can't take real punishment. And I've also had women who didn't want to submit to my authority but took it because they wanted my money. Stacy fell into that category. She sulked and made a big deal if I spanked her, even though she consented. I can be a dick, and I want things my way, but I'm not a total bastard–it's not like I forced her.

But Lexi's so different. First of all, she's more than a sexy body—she has a brain and a real personality. She's not the type to share her body just for a luxury apartment. I shouldn't be happy for her misfortune, but I know if she wasn't so desperate, she wouldn't have given me the time of day.

Maybe she never would have known she liked a dominant lover. Because I suspect I'm her first, and her body's responses to my authority surprise her. But I don't know how she'll feel about what happened last night in the light of day. Playful spanking's one thing, real punishment another. Just because she accepted it at the time doesn't mean it'll sit right with her the next day.

Which is why I should have stayed the night.

I hang around until my daughters are up, checking in with them about their plans for the day, then I take the additional cash Lexi needs to pay the whole debt off out of my safe and head over to the apartment.

* * *

I use my own key to get in and find her eating a bowl of cereal on the couch in a bralette and tiny pajama shorts. She looks good enough to eat.

"Good morning!" She jumps up in surprise, gathering up her cereal bowl, coffee mug and another plate from the coffee table and rushing to the kitchen to wash up. I should tell her I don't mind a few dishes—hell, Stacy trashed the place when she lived here—but the sight of her scurrying around to please me turns me on way too much.

"I'm sorry—I didn't expect to see you until this afternoon." She returns to the living room and runs her hands through her hair.

"Yeah. I wanted to see you."

Her eyes round, as if startled. Or is it hopeful? Either way, she cares. I'm sure of it. Just like seeing her rush to clean up pleases me, so does seeing the need in her eyes. She doesn't just want my money. She wants my approval. My attention.

There should be red flags flying everywhere–this is the opposite of what I wanted. What I thought I wanted. Except I like it too damn much to shut it down.

"Last night was intense." I open my arms.

"Intense, yeah," she breathes, stepping into me and resting her cheek against my chest.

I hear a sniff, and I go cold. Fuck. Did I take things too far? I ease her head away from my chest. "Are you crying?"

"No." She wipes her eye with the back of her hand. "I don't know what's wrong with me."

"Come here, *bambi*." I lead her to an armchair and pull her into my lap.

"It meant a lot to me that you accepted my punishment last night." I run my thumb along her cheek. "You took it so well. Was it too much? Are you okay?"

"I'm okay." Her eyes fill with tears again. "I'm sorry." She sniffs, swiping at her eyes with the back of her hand. "I'm not usually like this."

"Cry all you want," I tell her. "I gave the punishment, I can handle the tears."

This is part of the turn-on of being a dominant. It's backwards and wrong, but comforting her after I inflicted pain is as satisfying as delivering the pain. Aftercare is important and no less pleasurable. I cup the back of her neck and bring her head to my lips, brushing kisses along her hairline.

* * *

Lexi

I hide my face in Bobby's neck. I feel so raw emotionally. My life has been one giant upheaval this week, and I seriously don't know up from down. Head from tail.

I do know that it feels nice to be accepted like this, even when I'm a total mess. I like that he came over, anticipating that I might be mixed-up and feeling vulnerable after what went down between us.

"Were you really mad, Bobby? Or is it just...part of the game?"

He rubs slow circles over my back. "I was mad, yes." He coaxes my head away from his shoulder and cups my face. Finding my gaze, he holds it, making me flush.

He strokes my cheek with his thumb. "But I also have a streak of sadism in me. So spanking you was a pleasure for me."

It's not a huge revelation. I mean, I totally knew dominance was his kink from day one. I just don't know if he's trying to tell me something else. Like, if there's more, and this was just the tip of the iceberg.

He watches me closely. I get the feeling he's bracing for my reaction to his admission.

I swallow. "So..it turned you on?"

"Yes, the second you put yourself in position for me, all my piss-off was gone, and it became foreplay."

I examine my reaction to his words. I'm not offended. Not daunted. I appreciate his honesty. What's more, I like knowing what turns him on. That I pleased him just by accepting the punishment. That he's really not mad at all anymore. He's the opposite of mad.

He touches my cheek, and his gaze is warm. "You took it so well, beautiful girl. I loved it when you begged and pleaded but still held the position."

My face burns, but I don't look away. I'm incapable of

it, caught in his magnetic stare, the pull of his attention so addictive.

"It bonded me to you. Now I know you're really my girl. You're willing to do what it takes to make things right with me. I meant it last night when I said there is nothing in the world I wouldn't do for you. I loved the way you submitted to me for punishment."

"Did I really have a choice?"

He shrugs. "Definitely. Yeah. You always have a choice. You could walk out of here any time, sugar. You're not my prisoner. But if you stay, you follow my rules. That's our deal."

I take a deep breath. "There's this part of me that keeps freaking out about everything. Like this is just one giant mind-fuck, and I'm playing right into your hands. Did you ever see that movie *9½ Weeks*?"

"I thought it was hot."

I laugh. "Okay, so did I. But the message was that it was all wrong for her. And he was dangerous."

Bobby's brows drew together. "You think I'm a psychopath?"

Do I? No. He seems quite sane, actually. I shake my head. "No. I'm just confused. I've been mixed up all morning, that's why you caught me sitting around in my pajamas. Part of me feels bad about screwing up and getting in trouble, and then another part is a little upset that you actually punished me. And then still another part says none of it was real–it's just the way you like to have sex. And then the last piece of me says who really cares what you do, you just gave me a thousand bucks. If you want to take a belt to my ass and get us both off afterward, who am I to complain?"

Bobby's smile is sexy as hell. "I don't know, Lex. It is confusing. I like to be in charge of you. I like to punish—in the bedroom and for real. And real-life spanking is hotter to me, even when it isn't sexy in the moment. Does it make any sense to say that knowing you will submit to me in real life makes the sex steamier when we play?"

I relax. He's definitely sane. Hearing him articulate his fetish makes it obvious. He understands his quirk and doesn't believe punishing a woman for breaking rules is a God-given right afforded to men. Or even a normal, accepted behavior. He may be a dangerous criminal, but he's not deranged. He knows the line he walks.

In fact, it totally explains why he prefers the whole "arrangement" thing versus a real girlfriend.

He picks up my hand and interlaces his fingers over the tops of mine. "I know you liked some part of it, too," he murmurs.

I almost don't want to admit it, even though it's true. Because what if he gets even more intense with this? What if I no longer like it?

I lift our joined hands to my lips and kiss his fingers as my answer.

"So you're staying? You're still my girl?"

"Did you bring any money?" I ask with mock greediness. "No, just kidding. Bad joke. I sort of hate myself for using you like this."

"I don't hate myself for using you. At all." He waggles his eyebrows in an appreciative leer. "And yes, I brought the money. Go get dressed, and we'll take it down to the salon together."

I climb off his lap. "Do I have time for a quick shower?" I call over my shoulder as I pad to the bedroom.

"Do what you need to do."

I turn on the water and pop in the shower, making it quick, not wanting to keep him waiting. The heaviness and confusion that plagued me this morning is gone, and now as I shampoo my hair and shave my legs, a new excitement bubbles up. Bobby's still into me. My debt's getting paid off. And our honest conversation made me feel safe with him.

When I step out of the shower, I find Bobby sitting on the bathroom countertop, waiting.

I yank the towel from the rack. "Eek! You surprised me. I'm sorry, am I taking too long?"

As usual, he looks casually elegant, his khaki slacks crisply ironed, the short-sleeved button-down square cut at the bottom to wear untucked. "No, I just wanted to watch." His eyes rove across my wet shoulders, then skip down to my legs.

I drop the towel to give him the full view. "I'm yours to ogle."

He grins. "My buddy Dean just texted to say he has tickets to the Yankees game next week. You want to come?"

"I'd love to! Oh wait" I give him a coy look over my shoulder as I head out the door– "Why are you even asking? I thought I'm supposed to be available to you anytime you demand, unless I'm working."

He lunges and catches me around the waist before I make it out the door. Hauling me back, he puts his lips to my ear, nipping the shell of it before he growls, "Are you really going to tell me how to do my job?"

"No." I laugh.

He squeezes my ass, then cranes his neck to inspect my backside. I examined myself in the mirror this morning, fascinated with how quickly my ass recovered from punishment. Only a few red lines remain from my whipping.

"How is this beautiful ass today?"

I consider lying. I certainly don't want him to ever spank me harder than he did. But he seems so good at reading me, he'd probably know a fib when he heard it. "A little sting-y in places, but mostly fine," I admit.

He turns me to face him, squeezing and kneading my ass. "Does it scare you to hear I can't wait to do it again?" His voice is low and seductive. Giving pain definitely is his pleasure.

I swallow. My clenching, dripping core says no, regardless of my reluctance to admit anything to my demanding lover. "A little."

"I jacked off this morning to the memory of how you looked laid out on those pillows last night. All that sweet begging."

I flush, irrationally pleased by his turn-on.

He releases me and gives my ass a light tap. "Go on and get ready."

"Yes, Master." I laugh and go into the bedroom, pulling on a halter top and jeans.

"Mmm, mmm," Bobby says when he sees me. "Now that's what I'm talking about."

Chapter Ten

Lexi

L I finish up with my last client the next day and sweep up the hair on the floor.

It feels good to have paid off Arissa, and she's acting friendly to me, but honestly, I'm still hurt. I really, really hope I get the job at Stellar, so I can leave this place.

True to his word, Bobby had his secretary schedule an appointment for me with the EMDR therapist today, as well as a wax, manicure, and massage at a studio nearby. When I texted him to say thanks, he replied, *I take care of my girl.*

His girl.

The words produce an effervescent tension in me. Because I'm *not* his girl. Not really.

I'm his beck-and-call girl. Not his girlfriend.

I'm his available-for-sex girl. Not someone he spends the night with.

Crap. And this growing disappointment that we aren't and can't be more signals that I'm developing feelings for him. Which I never planned to do.

I put the broom away, and my client gets up. The door swings open, and an imposing, dark figure crosses the frame. Bobby's carrying a bouquet of orange roses, and he looks like a million bucks, as usual.

My heart leaps at the sight of him, adrenaline erasing the weariness of working on my feet all day. The ache and stiffness in my knee. Ondrea has gone home for the day, and my client and I are the only other people in the salon. I beam a smile and hold up my finger to indicate I'll be done in a minute.

He nods, leaning up against the wall, his arms folded across his chest, the flowers tucked under one arm.

"Ooh, who is that?" Joanna, my client, asks.

I smile. "He's my date."

Yeah. For all the stern lecturing I gave myself about squelching my feelings for Bobby, there's no denying the level of excitement fluttering in my chest.

"Ooh," Joanna murmurs appreciatively. "Lucky you."

After she pays and leaves, I start to pull off my smock.

"Wait just a second, beautiful. I'm here to collect on one of those haircuts," Bobby rumbles.

"Oh!" I re-tie the smock strings. "Okay, come on over."

He sits in my chair, gazing at me in the mirror with a predatory look. I spin him around to face me, moving in close to straddle one of his knees as I run my fingers through his hair. "Just a trim?" I purr.

He grabs my ass and kneads it, his grasp possessive. "Yeah. Whatever you think is best."

I pick up his hand and tug it. "Come on, I'll shampoo you."

Leading him to the sinks, I offer a chair and recline it, warming the water to the perfect temperature before I use the gentle spray nozzle to wet his hair. Something about serving him this way makes the entire experience erotic for me, the sense of power similar to when I give him a blowjob.

I take my time, massaging his scalp with shampoo, the pads of my fingers becoming a sensual tool to stimulate his pleasure, his sighs of appreciation fueling my desire to please. By the time I've lathered, rinsed and repeated, a steady pulse of desire thrums through me.

"Lexi." He sounds gruff, "If you don't sit on my cock soon, I'm going to bust."

"Bust, huh?" I make my voice seductive as I lift the back of his chair to bring him upright and wrap a towel around his head. I walk around the front of him and kneel, unbuttoning his pants and lowering the zipper.

"Huh uh," he says, when I free his length and lean forward to take it into my mouth. "I said *sit on my cock*." He pulls out a condom and sheaths his straining length.

"Right. You have to be in charge, don't you?" I stand.

"Come here." He lifts my skirt and pulls me forward to straddle him. "It's not that you don't give the very best head," he says, as if he's afraid he offended me. He strokes the lips of my pussy through my panties, then slides them off and dips two fingers into my juices.

I gasp, jerking at the shock of pleasure rippling through me.

"It's just that I really need to be in you right now." He cups my ass and pulls my hips, so my exposed pussy rubs over the side of his cock.

"Yes," I pant, grasping his member and lifting my hips up to guide him in.

He closes his eyes, holding my butt cheeks and pulling me against him with a slamming force, rocking his hips up each time to thrust.

We find a rhythm together, me sliding forward and

back, trying to take him deeper every time. It feels wonderful. Seeing the lust in his expression empowers me.

At this rate, I won't last long. "Oh God," I moan.

"Lexi..."

The sound of my name uttered with such appreciation stokes my passion even more, and I claw at his back, my own animal aggression matching his.

"Please?" I whimper.

"Go ahead, baby," he urges, and I buck at the command, the words all I need to reach the summit and topple over the edge into ecstasy. Shuddering all around him, I come, stilling to relish the sensation of having him so deep inside me. When the room stops spinning and my breath quiets, I open my eyes to gaze at the expressive lines of his face.

He wears his satisfied-cat look, heavy-lidded and sexy. "Now I can stand you cutting my hair."

I scramble off him, the task made difficult by the post-climactic languor. He helps me to my feet and hands me the discarded panties, disposes of the condom, then follows me back to my chair, looking as relaxed as I feel.

I drape him in a cutting cape. His hair is simple to cut, but I take my time, wanting to get it perfect.

His phone rings just as I finish. He looks at the name and stands from the chair before I have a chance to brush him off and remove the drape. "I need to take this." He strides toward the back of the salon.

I sweep up the hair and throw a load of towels in the wash. Then I follow in the direction Bobby went to retrieve his cape and clean him off. He holds up his finger with a frown when I find him.

"I'm just going to grab this cape," I whisper, darting forward to pull it off him.

"Don't." His tone is sharp enough to make me jump. I

spin on my heel and retreat, more offended than I'd like to be.

I go to the laundry room even though there's nothing to be done there.

I stand at the washing machine, not seeing anything when Bobby's strong arms close around me from behind. Not rough or demanding. Conciliatory.

"I'm sorry. I didn't mean to be an asshole." He runs his hands up and down my arms, across my waist. He turns me to face him. "I was a dick. I shouldn't have barked." He cups my face. "Forgive me, Lex?"

My nose burns unaccountably, and I nod.

"It was...business. You don't ever want to be in the position of overhearing anything that makes you useful to the feds and a liability to the Family. I'm trying to protect you, *bambi*."

I bob my head. "I understand."

"That's my girl." He brushes his lips across mine then kisses them softly, coaxing a response from me. When he pulls away he strokes the back of his finger up my neck and under my chin. "Can I make it up to you?"

* * *

Bobby

I lift Lexi to sit on the washing machine and spread her knees wide. Words are cheap. Orgasms go farther when it comes to apologizing. I pull her ass right up to the edge and tug the gusset of her panties to the side.

"I'm gonna make you come so hard you forget everything but the fact that I own this sweet little body." I lick into her, taking my time tracing around her labia, then rolling my tongue over her clit. When she gets juicy and starts moaning, I slide two fingers inside her with one hand. With the other, I reach up and grasp her throat. I don't squeeze—I would never do that without a discussion first, but I give her the idea of restraint. The sensation of being owned.

Clearly it's a turn-on because she goes wild, undulating her hips to take my fingers deeper and making the cutest greedy sounds in her throat.

I stop stroking over her G-spot and instead, start finger-fucking her, the pads of my two fingers bumping that sensitive bundle of nerves every time I hit her inner wall.

She whines and moans, her knees clamping around my shoulders. I apply my tongue to her clit at the same time I pump my digits into her. It only takes a few seconds before she's screaming my name, her tight channel squeezing and pulsing around my fingers.

"That's it, *cara mia*." I ease my fingers out, pull her off the washing machine and turn her around. "Take those panties off for me."

She's dazed but manages to follow my instructions as I pull out another condom, and roll it over my cock, wishing for once I could skip it and get the full sensation of her hot pussy enveloping my bare cock.

I press against her entrance, groaning as she welcomes me in, her plump folds parting with the sweetest sensation as they close around the head of my member.

I grip both her elbows and pull them back, pressing her chest down on the washing machine as I pump into her.

"Who do you belong to, beautiful girl?"

"Ahh..."

I fuck her harder. "Who makes you come, sweetheart?"

"You do!" she gasps.

This time, I finish, slamming my pelvis against hers

until I come with a roar. "Come, Lexi!" I command, and she bucks, her body obedient to my will, her muscles tightening around my cock in a pulsing crescendo.

Even after I pull out, remove the condom and zip up my pants, I hold her immobilized against the washing machine.

Tracing a finger down her butt crack, I touch her little pink pucker. "Has anyone ever taken you here before?"

"No," she pants.

"No? With an ass this sweet? That's a travesty." I press my finger more insistently. She tightens against the intrusion. "Spread your legs wide, baby."

She whimpers softly and opens wider.

I bring my fingers up, lightly spanking her pussy.

She moans.

I repeat the action, spanking her pussy again and again, delighted that despite her whimpers of protest, she holds perfectly still for it. I dip my thumb into her juices to lubricate it, then push it against her anus, gaining entry as I slide two fingers into her pussy at the same time. I fingerfuck her, first pressing my thumb, then the two fingers, alternating holes as her mewls of protest and need grow louder.

She screams as she bucks in a fourth orgasm, giving a sob of relief as it shakes her. I ease my fingers out and help her into her panties, then flip her skirt down. Turning her to face me, I kiss her.

"Are we good?"

She nods. Her eyes are dilated, and she looks drunk, her knees wobbly beneath her.

I put my arm around her waist and guide her toward the door. "What else do you need to do to close up?"

She looks around blankly. "Uh...just lock up, I guess."

I wash my hands in the sink and stop by her station. "Where's your purse?"

She gives her head a shake, as if to recover her senses. "Oh! Got it." She opens a drawer and retrieves the purse, taking out her keys. She sets the alarm, and we exit. When she selects the correct key, I take it from her hands and lock the door.

"I'll drive you home, but I can't stay. That call was bad news."

She searches my face, her sharp intelligence returning, but she knows better than to ask.

When we reach the apartment, I walk her to the door, and pull her into my arms, kissing her. I sense her disappointment at ending the date early, but she doesn't complain. Even though I already gave her twenty-five hundred for her salon rent, I stuff some more cash in her purse without her noticing. Spoiling this woman is my new favorite thing.

"Goodnight, baby. Be good."

She wraps her arms around my neck and offers her lips, but the line between her brows as she turns away tells me not to go.

Fuck. I wish I could stay. I really do. But the Feds just subpoenaed all my financial records. That's on top of the IRS audit.

The mayor called five times.

So even though I sense Lexi pulling back, which means running off on her tonight is a mistake, I kiss her one more time and leave.

Chapter Eleven

Lexi

Two days later, I walk out of the therapist's office with a bounce in my step. Bobby was right—it seems like the EMDR completely liberated me from the trauma of the car accident. I sat in the therapist's office and described the accident, moment by moment, all the while moving my eyes slowly from side to side. The therapist had me imagine the disturbing images of the event and conjure the feelings. When I stayed with the eye movements, all the terror lost its power over me.

Although I made a follow up appointment, I left completely transformed, so I doubt I need any further help. As if to confirm my positivity, when I check my voicemail afterward, I find a message from human resources at Stellar saying they want to schedule an interview.

"Yes!" I whisper out loud as I walk to the bus stop.

I dial the number, and by a third miracle, schedule the interview for Tuesday afternoon, a few hours after the massage Bobby's secretary set up for me. I'll be relaxed and ready to impress!

I call Gina. "Guess what?"

"What?"

"I got an interview for the job!"

"Awesome! That's fantastic, you deserve it, girl!"

"I'm so excited. And it just so happens that Bobby set up a massage for me that day, so I'll be cool, calm and collected."

"A massage, huh? I love that for you." Gina sounds impressed.

"I know. He takes good care of me. Did I tell you he paid off my rent at the salon, too?"

"What did I tell you? He's a keeper."

"Well, not really."

"Why, what do you mean?"

"Nothing. Just that he's not available. Unless I want to be essentially his call girl for the rest of my life."

"Oh. Gotcha. I'm sorry." She's silent a moment, and I wish I hadn't mentioned it. The reminder of my non-relationship status with Bobby is a bit of a downer on an otherwise bright day. "That kinda sucks, doesn't it?" It's like it finally hit her that her fix for me–setting me up with a sugar daddy–had a catch.

"Yeah."

"Well...don't worry about it for now. Just enjoy being treated like a princess. You deserve a little pampering after all you've been through over the last year."

"Yeah, thanks. That's kind of what I arrived at, too. It's good for now. Just not a permanent thing. Okay, I gotta go. I should call Bobby."

"All right, take care, babe."

"You too. Bye!"

I end the call with Gina and dial Bobby's number, my

pulse picking up speed, the way it always does when I interact with him.

"Hey, doll."

Wings in my chest flap at the sound of his deep rumble. "Hey! Thank you so much for setting up the therapy appointment for me. I feel completely transformed. What a difference!"

"That's great. Glad to hear it."

"And I just found out I got the job interview—you know, for that trainer position?"

"Of course I remember—the reason you took portfolio pictures. Congratulations. When is it?"

"Tuesday afternoon."

"Fantastic. I'll take you shopping for clothes, unless you already know what you want to wear."

Um, wow. This guy. He really does love to play sugar daddy. And I am not complaining. "No—uh—I'd love to go shopping with you. Thanks!"

"Listen, *bambi*, I wish I could take you out tonight to celebrate, but I'm up to my ears in shit right now. I will try to get over later, if I can."

"Sure...no problem." I'm irrationally disappointed. I didn't expect him to take me out to celebrate, but now that he expressed the desire, I totally want it. Miss it. Need it.

"Okay, I'll text you if I can make it. Bye, doll."

I end the call quickly because the disappointment hits me like a steamroller, flattening my mood. I draw a deep breath and exhale.

Gah. I'm getting way too needy with this guy. Our agreement was very specific–he's not my boyfriend. I don't get to make demands or expect boyfriend-like things from him.

He's the boss. I'm essentially his employee.

But I can't seem to separate emotion from sex. I'm definitely falling for Bobby. Or I want to. And I can already see the heartbreak looming when this ends.

* * *

Lexi

After work, I take myself to L'amore, the restaurant where Bobby told the staff I could dine on his dime. I figure Bobby wanted to take me out, so I'm letting him.

I've never dined alone before, especially not at an upscale place with "love" in the name, but I hold my head high and muscle through it. The maitre d' and the waiter remember me without my reminder, which goes a long way to making me feel comfortable.

I order a glass of wine and a Caesar salad with chicken and add two new photos to my Instagram page–Lexi Styles Hair. I try to post a few photos of new haircuts or highlights every week. My Instagram account is actually how I found out about the Stellar position. Someone at Stellar had seen my latest reel and sent me a message inviting me to apply.

It sort of felt meant-to-be, but I'm trying not to get my hopes up.

The wine is delicious, and the salad fills me up. I'm lonely, but trying to feel okay with being alone. This is what it means to belong to Bobby. I'm at his beck and call, but he's not available to me.

It makes me even more glad I "let" him treat me here tonight.

If eating here is one of my perks, I need to be cashing in on it since I don't get the full package.

I shove the pity-party thoughts from my mind and focus on enjoying dinner.

It was still a great day, regardless of the availability of my...what is he to me? Boyfriend? Owner? I prefer owner to boyfriend, actually.

When it's time to leave, the waiter assures me that my meal is taken care of, but I leave a big cash tip, since they made me feel like a princess.

When I get home, I find a bouquet of lavender roses in a vase waiting outside my door. Attached is a note of congratulations from Bobby. My eyes mist, and I wipe all resentments from my mind. I don't need to be a glass half empty kind of girl. Or look a gift horse in the mouth. Or whatever other metaphor fits the situation.

I text him to thank him for the roses and let him know I ate at L'amore. I try not to feel disappointed when he doesn't respond. At eleven, I give up waiting for word from him and change into my pajamas, turn out the lights and go to bed.

I wake to the sound of Bobby's voice. "Hey, baby." He climbs over the covers, reaching for me. His hands find my breasts, stroke down my body.

"Hey," I murmur groggily as my body warms under his lustful stroking.

He slides one hand down the front of my pajama shorts to cup my mons. "You're getting a spanking tonight," he murmurs in my ear.

I go still. "What did I do?"

"Nothing." His fingers glide over my wet pussy, and I relax. "I just want to smack that sweet ass of yours." He rolls me to my belly, pinning me down with his body. "Are you going to be a good girl and let me, or do I have to wait until you're naughty?"

I moan. His words make me squirm, Or maybe it's his hands. My body ignites under his possessive handling.

"You're the boss," I purr. There's a certain power in being asked, an excitement at giving him something he wants, combined with the thrill of fear at knowing beyond any shadow of a doubt he enjoys delivering pain.

He burrows his thick fingers into my hair, massaging my scalp before closing his fist and tugging my head back. "Mmm. That's right, I am the boss of you, aren't I, sweet girl?"

"Yes, Master," I moan.

He nips my ear with his teeth. "I love it when you call me that."

I love it when he says, *I love it*. His approval excites me the same way the words "good girl" make me warm and tingly.

He climbs off and pulls the covers back. My heart rate increases when he lifts my hips into the air, so I'm on my knees with my face and chest still pressed into the pillow.

Bobby strokes his large hand over the curve of my ass. "Who do you belong to?"

"You."

He comes off the bed and stands beside it. "Are you mine to do anything I want to?"

I turn my head to face the direction of his voice, blinking into the darkness. "Yes."

"To fuck any way I want to?"

"Yes."

He moves near my head, and I hear the sound of a zipper. "Open your mouth."

I reach for his cock, but he catches my wrist.

"No hands," he murmurs, his voice low and sultry. "I want to fuck your mouth."

I find the head of his cock with my lips, and he pushes in.

"That's it, pretty girl. You're so perfect. So willing."

I make a muffled sound of assent.

He cradles the back of my head and plunges slowly in and out of my mouth, controlling me completely.

* * *

Bobby

I'm only a few strokes from orgasm. Lexi looks so hot with her face turned to the side, her pouty lips wrapped around my cock. Not wanting to come yet, I pull out of her mouth.

"Present your ass to me," I command.

The way she instantly complies makes me dizzy with lust for her, the power and euphoria of dominance surging through my veins like a powerful drug. Her moan makes me draw a quick breath.

I slap her backside, my palm having perfect aim, even in the dim light. I slap again lightly, since it's for pleasure, not punishment, and I want to ease her into it. I continue with slightly harder spanks while she makes little gasps and waggles her ass as if tempting me to slap her harder.

After a few dozen strokes, I increase the intensity, slowing down to give her time to digest the sting.

"I love the sound of your cries," I tell her.

She makes an incoherent noise.

I slap a little harder. "I love to see my handprints on your ass. To leave my mark."

She moans.

"Can you believe it's an expression of my love, Lex?"

She stills, as if listening.

I crawl over her, gripping her hair in my fist again and pulling her head back. I speak in her ear between clenched teeth. "It drives me crazy when you give yourself to me like this."

Her cry of excitement sends me over the edge, and I nudge her thighs wider with my knees and sheath my cock, shoving into her without preamble. I knew she'd be more than ready for me, the plumped and swollen folds of her pussy open like a flower. I lose myself in her delicious heat, my eyes rolling back as all rational thought disappears.

Lexi's moaning brings me back, and I reach forward, cupping my palm under her chin to lift her head, bowing her back as I continue to slam into her.

She gives a surprised mewl. The angle of her hips gives me a perfect thrust toward her g-spot.

"Who gets to fuck you, Lex?"

"You do, Master!" She sounds desperate with need.

I come, losing my mind again as the release explodes through my every sense. "Oh...*God!*" I shout.

"Yes!" she screams.

I release her chin and push her into the bed at her nape, restraining her as she jerks and convulses under me in her own beautiful climax.

I hold our bodies locked together that way, my cock still embedded deep within her, her ass still warm from the spanking, her upper body restrained under my palm.

I stroke slowly in and out, caressing her with my cock, or maybe better put, caressing my cock with her delicious heat.

She makes a contented noise, and I pull out and remove the condom, tossing it in the trash. I settle beside her, drawing her into my arms.

"Thank you, Lexi. You are the best thing in my life right

now." I push away the comparisons because I definitely don't want to be thinking about the shitstorm the Feds are bringing down on me. Lexi relieved every ounce of tension I brought over.

I drift into sleep with my girl locked in my embrace, right where I want to be.

Chapter Twelve

I wake to the feel of Lexi's nails scratching my back. "Mmm," I murmur.

"Did you mean to spend the night?"

"Yes." I'm not really sure why I broke my rules last night. Other than the simple truth. "I wanted to be with you."

I should get up, put my dick away and hightail it out of here before either of us catch any more feelings for each other. Because that's what's happening here.

It's definitely happening on my part, and I'm fairly certain Lexi's been there for a while. I should keep the boundaries clear. This is an arrangement, not a relationship. She's my plaything. That's the way I like things.

My body refuses to move, though. I love being here with her far too much. There's something so refreshing about Lexi. She's genuine. Honest.

She runs her perfect salon nails up my back again. "It's nice to wake up with you." There's a shyness in her voice that makes me want to reassure her.

"Yeah. I like it, too." I roll on top of her and kiss her neck. "You're special, Lex. I really like you."

"You *like* me?" She pushes me away with a playfully exaggerated sense of offense. "And spanking me is a sign of your love, right?"

"Uh oh." I sit up and drag her over my lap. "You're not sulking are you?" I deliver a flurry of spanks on her beautiful backside, loving the way her cheeks flatten and spring back under my palm.

"Ack! No!" She reaches back to protect herself.

I lean over and kiss one cheek, then the other, then I release her. "Good," I say. "Because that would tell me you need more."

She blinks those beautiful baby blues at me. I love the way she trains them on me, completely surrendered, attuned to my mood, my commands. She's a perfect submissive.

"What do you like for breakfast?" She rolls away and climbs off the bed.

I turn lazily to watch her. "Want to go out for something? What time do you work?"

"Not until eleven. But I want to make you breakfast. What do you eat?"

Aw, damn. *She wants to make me breakfast.* I can't stop the broad smile from stretching across my face. As much as I like being in charge, being in control, it's damn refreshing to be with someone who wants to do something for me, and *not* just because I told her to.

"Anything you're making, sugar."

"You're easy? No diet restrictions? Anything you hate?"

"Nope. Bring it on. You make it, I'll eat it."

She throws on a short robe and bounces off, looking enthusiastic.

I find my way to the shower, still groggy from lack of sleep and the relaxation of good sex just a few hours before. I didn't arrive until after three a.m., and then we spent another hour making love. Well, maybe *love* isn't the right term for what we did. But the after-effects sure as hell feel like love.

I take a long shower. When I get out, I smell bacon and something savory. After dressing, I head into the kitchen. "Whatcha making?" I wrap my arms around her from behind.

"I made a goat cheese, mushroom and asparagus frittata, with bacon on the side."

"No shit." I'm impressed. "I didn't know you cooked.'

She flashes her model-perfect smile, beaming. "I would've made you coffee, but I haven't figured out your fancy espresso machine yet."

"Aw, sweetheart. You should've asked me sooner. I didn't know you were doing without java." I show her how to use the thousand dollar DeLonghi espresso machine, making her a latte and two shots of espresso for myself.

"Do you mind if I take the world's fastest shower before we eat?"

I kiss her forehead. "Make it snappy," I murmur, only because I love to watch her scramble to please. I could care less if she takes her time and our breakfast gets cold. I'm not much of a breakfast guy, anyway. "I'm timing you!" I call after her back as she dashes toward the master bathroom. I sit to drink my espresso at the glass table situated near the wall-sized windows overlooking the city. She set the table for us like a perfect little 1950's housewife.

My ex-wife did all these things, too. We started off great, but after the first five years, resentments grew between both of us. They grew and grew until we couldn't stand each other. She became a ball-buster. I stayed away from the house. We're much happier divorced. I pay her alimony, and she never complains anymore.

Financial arrangements make everything easier. Clear expectations.

She returns with her thick hair dripping, in a short denim skirt and tight t-shirt.

I glance at my watch and whistle. "Five minutes, three seconds. I think you deserve a reward for that."

"Oh yeah?" she purrs, coming to stand over me and pressing her cleavage in my face.

I nip at her breast. "And for that outfit..."

She gives a husky laugh and moves away, going to the kitchen to pick up the casserole dish with the frittata and bringing it to the table. "Help yourself. I'll be right back with the bacon."

She returns with the bacon and slides into the chair next to me. "This is an incredible view. I really enjoy staying here, Bobby. Thanks."

"I love having you here, *bambina*," I take a bite of the frittata. "Mmm, this is amazing!"

Lexi looks happy. Genuinely happy. I haven't seen her so relaxed and content before. It makes me want to do everything in my power to keep that smile on her face.

I take a second helping because it's truly delicious and also because I want her to know how much I appreciate her efforts. When we finish, I help carry the dishes into the kitchen and put them in the dishwasher.

"So, when should we go shopping for your interview clothes? Tonight after you get off?"

She lights up. "Yes! That sounds great!"

I smile. "Okay, I'll pick you up. And I want to see the portfolio you put together for this job."

"You do?" She sounds surprised.

"Yeah. Is it here? Bring it to me."

She gives me a curious look over her shoulder as she retreats to the bedroom. When she returns, she has a sleek black photo album. "This is my look-book, but I submitted a digital slide show with the application."

I leaf through the pages, admiring each hairstyle. "Who took the photos?"

"Well, I did. I wish I could have had them professionally done because you can see here how the shadows fall on her face." She traces a finger across the model's face. "I didn't have the right lighting."

"Next time we'll get you a professional shoot, sugar. Your work deserves to be showcased with the best tools available to us."

"We?" she asks faintly. She's staring at me with an odd look on her face.

"What?"

She gives her head a quick shake. "Nothing. Just that sometimes I wish you were more of an asshole."

"Oh, I am an asshole, believe me," I say lightly, but I sense a wistfulness in Lexi, and she doesn't smile.

Damn. She's definitely getting attached. I shouldn't have spent the night. I should stay away for a few days.

Except that idea literally makes me want to punch a wall.

* * *

Lexi

"What do you think of this one?" I prance out of the dressing cubicle in a fitted purple miniskirt, wide black belt and black cap-sleeved top that makes my boobs look amazing.

Bobby lounges on one of the benches in the dressing room, looking casually elegant in one of his designer suits. Shopping is foreplay, and I'm about two seconds away from dragging him into a cubicle and dropping to my knees to suck his cock because he bought everything I showed the slightest interest in, and more.

He gives me a heavy-lidded gaze. "I think, if I were God, I would ordain that this song be playing every time you entered into my visual field in a short skirt."

I laugh, listening to hear what song played on the mall speakers. It's "Sex and Candy" by Marcy Playground.

"Sweetheart, those legs ought to be illegal. In fact," he motions to my outfit. "We'll take those clothes, but you are not wearing them to your interview."

"Oh yeah?" I strut slowly to where he sits. "What am I wearing to the interview?"

He smirks. "I'm not sure, but I think you already have something in mind. You just keep dragging me around to turn me on with your dress up show."

I laugh. "I can't get anything by you, can I?" At least he didn't accuse me of working him for the clothes, which was also true, and I know he understands that perfectly.

"All right, baby, I'm almost out of cash." He pulls out three hundred dollar bills. "Where do you want to spend these?"

"Shoe store," I say without hesitation. I gesture at my outfit. "Should I get these?"

"Yes." He rakes his gaze up and down me appreciatively. "I thought I already said so."

"Sorry, boss." I wink as I turn to strut back to the cubicle and change out of the clothes.

In the shoe department, I pick out a pair of wedge sandals and a pair of strappy platform heels. "How much is left?" I smile like a spoiled child after he pays for the clothes and shoes.

"Sixty bucks." He folds the bills and slides them into my bra. "But I'm all shopped out. Let's go, *bambina*."

"Okay, boss." I traipse beside him, giddy with the new purchases and the attention of my lover. I hook my arm through his. "May I make you dinner?"

He looks down at me, thoughtfully. When he hesitates, I brace against feeling rejected, but then he says, "Sure."

We walk to his car, but he hesitates when he unlocks the door. "Why don't you drive?"

"What?"

"Have you driven at all since your accident?"

"No," I admit. My heart is already beating faster at the thought of it. It's true I wasn't scared riding in his car as a passenger today, but that doesn't mean I won't freak out if I get behind a wheel.

"Get in." He waves me toward the driver's seat. "I want you to drive. Let's test your EMDR session."

I climb in, feeling shaky. I adjust the seat and mirrors, trying to get everything just perfect, as if it would make driving easier. Taking a deep breath, I start the Porsche, check for cars in the mirror and pull out into the stream of traffic. Neither of us speak for the next ten minutes as I navigate my way through the city streets, but after a while, I relax my hands on the steering wheel.

I nod. "It's okay," I say on an exhale. "I'm doing okay."

I experience no panic, and with each mile I drive, it gets easier. By the time I pull into the underground parking garage at my building, I feel more confident about driving. I find a parking spot and turn off the car, turning to grin at Bobby. "Just like riding a bike," I declare.

"Good job, baby. I'm proud of you."

Pleasure blooms in my chest at his praise. I take his arm feeling half-giddy with affection.

When we arrive at the apartment, he follows me into the kitchen. "May I help?"

"Do you cook?" It's weird how little I know about the man who occupies so many of my thoughts.

He grins. "I'm not bad in a kitchen. Better on a grill."

My heart pinches. These glimpses of domesticity cause me pain. God, am I starting to wish for the full deal? For everything? I didn't go out looking to get married or settle down. Bobby's just supposed to be a job.

I pull some white roughy fillets out of the freezer and pop them in a bowl of warm water to thaw. "Actually, I have this covered. You could just set the table?"

"Sure thing," He empties his pockets onto the countertop before taking out placemats and napkins.

The phone on the counter buzzes, and I reach for it automatically, picking it up to check the text message. Only when I read the words *What's the latest with the Feds?* do I realize it's not my phone, and I definitely shouldn't have looked.

"What are you doing?" The ice in Bobby's tone turns me cold. He stands in the kitchen doorway, his gaze sharp, expression rigid. Jesus. Does he think I'm spying?

I drop the phone like a hot potato. "Oh God." I shake my hands as if to remove all traces of his phone from them. "I didn't— I wasn't—"

He steps forward, looking every inch the dangerous mobster. His face is dark, but the stunned expression conveys something more—betrayal.

A spike of genuine terror shoots through me. Fuck. He actually thinks I'm an informer, or a rat or whatever they call them.

* * *

Bobby

The color drains from Lexi's face. "I thought it was my phone! It beeped, and I just picked it up to check the message. We have the same phones and the same beeps."

I blow out my breath. Is she telling the truth? She certainly looks terrified. But a snitch who got caught would be scared.

Her eyes fill with tears. "I'm not a rat or a Fed. I'm not wearing a wire, I swear to you."

I scrub a hand across my face. *Cristo.* This shit with the Feds is getting to me. I definitely didn't get enough sleep last night.

Of course, Lexi's not a rat. I would've known if there was something off about her. I have excellent instincts about people. My muscles loosen.

"Okay. It's okay, baby. I'm sorry I overreacted." I pull her into my arms. She's trembling, which makes me feel like a *stronzo* for barking at her. I cup the back of her head to angle her face to mine and give her a hard kiss. "I didn't mean to scare you."

She lets out a relieved laugh. "You scared the crap out of me."

I kiss her forehead, her temple.

Because I'm a sick fuck, her trembling relief makes my dick thicken in my trousers. I pick up her wrists, turning her slowly to face the counter. Pressing her hands down on the granite, I pull up her skirt and lower her panties.

"But snooping isn't allowed, Lexi." I reach for a wooden spoon.

She whimpers but pushes her ass out, offering it to me.

I pepper her backside lightly with spanks, and she holds still, gasping, but not squirming. Seeing the bottle of olive oil standing on the counter, I reach for it, pouring a little in my palm. I rub it over her cheeks, then slap, enjoying the stingy-ness the oil helps to impart. I dip my finger in the oil and slide it between her cheeks, circling her anus.

"I think you deserve a little back door punishment." I press my finger in.

"Oh God," she moans.

"That's right, *bambina*. This is what happens to this beautiful ass of yours when you've been bad." I plunge my finger into the knuckle, then withdraw it and repeat the action.

"Ohhh..."

With my free hand, I spank the back of her thigh. "Are you going to be a good girl and take it?" I spank her again. My thumb swipes between her legs, and I find her dripping wet.

"You're the boss." She looks over her shoulder at me with heat in her azure gaze.

"That's right, pretty girl." I ease my finger out and take her elbow to pull her toward the living room. I lead her to the bolstered arm of the sofa. "Bend over, *bambi*."

She folds her torso down, so her bare ass is raised and exposed.

"Do not move from this position." I go to the kitchen to retrieve the olive oil, which I liberally use on her anus and my shaft, while she shivers in anticipation. I rub the head of my cock against her entrance and press. She tightens against the intrusion.

"Open for me, Lex," I encourage. "Push back like you're bearing down."

She obeys immediately, seemingly as eager for this as I am. Or maybe she's just eager to please. Either way, she's ready for me.

I ease into her, giving her time to get used to my girth and the unusual invasion. She pants and moans, but remains perfectly still, allowing me to penetrate, centimeter by centimeter. Reaching around the front, I tease her clit, flicking it as I begin to withdraw and press in again.

"Oh God!" I moan.

"That's right, beautiful. You're taking it in the ass tonight." I may sound like an asshole, but I maintain the utmost care in keeping my in and out strokes gliding smoothly, wanting it to be a good experience for her.

"Bobby," she whimpers.

"That's it, baby. You're taking it like a good girl."

"Please?" she begs.

"Please what, baby?"

"Please, please, please." She thrashes her head from side to side.

I increase my speed, still being careful to keep my thrusts direct. She presses her fingers over mine, shoving them inside her pussy. I fingerfuck her, and she lets out a high-pitched cry that goes on and on until it draws a climax from me. I keep my fingers moving inside her as I press my cock deep in her ass and come.

After I spend, I ease out, withdrawing my fingers and gently stroking over her wet pussy. I cover her body with mine, wrapping my free arm around her torso and kissing her neck.

"Don't move, baby." I get up to wash up in the bathroom. I return with a wet washcloth, which I use to clean her before pulling up her panties and smoothing down her skirt. "Come here." I lift her torso and turn her to face me. She falls into my arms, and I sense her trembling. I kiss the top of her head and hold her for a moment, then scoop her into my arms and carry her to the sofa, where I sit with her cradled in my lap. I grab the soft throw blanket from the back of the sofa and wrap her in it.

"Are you okay?"

She nods against my shoulder.

"Did you get off?"

She lifts her head. "Yes. Well, I feel like I did. Except I sort of skipped the part where my muscles tighten up. I was afraid it would hurt to clench my...um...anus," she admits.

I smile. "Maybe it would have."

"But you more than satisfied me."

I grin. "Good."

She holds my gaze. "You really thought I was a snitch there for a minute, didn't you?"

"No, *bambi*." I shake my head, not wanting to go down this road with her. "Your behavior surprised me until you explained it."

"But you thought I was an informer, didn't you?" she presses. "I saw the look on your face."

I study her. "I just couldn't understand why you would snoop, that's all."

"What would you have done if I didn't explain?"

"Lex," I admonish. "Let's not go there. I trust you. I will buy you a new phone case, so you don't get confused again."

She continues to observe me without speaking.

"I'm sorry I scared you. I truly am."

She shivers and snuggles against me. "You did. Just for a minute, though."

Chapter Thirteen

Bobby

The following Sunday, I pick up Lexi and drive her to Yankee stadium for the game. I already know I'm in too deep. I'm indulging in more than the pleasure of her body. I'm acting like she's a girlfriend. This goes beyond treating her to dinner or shopping. I'm actually bringing her to a social engagement. With a guy from the outfit.

I'm crossing lines here left and right and can't seem to stop myself.

Still, Lexi looks gorgeous in a halter top and capris, her hair twisted up in a messy French twist, and I can't bring myself to regret bringing her along. Being with her makes me happy. Truly happy. Possibly for the first time, ever.

I somehow manage to find parking close to the stadium, and we pick up tickets from Will Call. When we get to our seats, I find Dean with his wife and baby. Looks like I wasn't the only one who wanted to be with his woman today.

"Dean, you brought the family!" I shake Dean's hand.

"And you brought your...uh" he waves a hand in the air as if trying to conjure the right word.

"This is Lexi. Hi Jessie." I kiss Dean's wife on both cheeks as Dean shakes Lexi's hand. I touch the baby's head. "It's great to see you out and about, Olive." I lean down to see her big brown eyes. Jessie bounces Olive up and down, and the baby smiles at me.

"Aw, she likes you!" Jessie says.

"Of course she likes me, she knows I'm family." I grin. "Jessie, Dean, this is Lexi."

Lexi and Jessie greet each other, and we settle into the stadium seats, the men sitting beside each other, with the women on the outside.

"Well, they're getting the hits they need, if they can only get some pitching," Dean says.

"Yeah, they've got the starting pitching, if they can only get some relief. They blew another save last night—it's the tenth one they've blown this month."

Jessie extricates the baby from the carrier and drapes the fabric over her shoulder, pulling up her shirt to nurse.

"Don't look at my wife's breasts." Dean's warning is probably only a half-joke.

I hold up my hands. "I wouldn't dream of it." I reach out to squeeze Lexi's thigh.

When the little one finishes nursing, Dean takes her from Jessie, holding her to his shoulder and patting her back. He's already an old pro handling her.

It almost makes me miss having little ones. *Almost.* But those days were so long ago, I've blocked out how intense fatherhood is when you have young children. The twins made everything twice as intense.

"So how is fatherhood? What do the two of you do all day, just sit around and stare at your little princess?"

Jessie laughs. "Pretty much. Dean made me quit work five months into the pregnancy, and he has flexible hours, so we're home a lot. This is an exciting outing for me."

Lexi leans forward, finally relaxed enough to join the conversation. "What did you do before you quit?"

"Nursing assistant."

Lexi launches into easy conversation with Jessie, flashing her beautiful smile. I can't help but notice how easily she fits in with family. I never in a million years could've brought Stacy to an event like this and expect her to make intelligent conversation.

"I'm blessed." Dean sounds truly religious about it as he gazes at his wife.

"Jessie, may I hold her?" I lean across Dean to look at her. "I'm good with babies, I promise."

Jessie smiles. "Sure."

Dean carefully transfers the little bundle to me, and I place her on her back on my lap, cradling her tiny head in my palms, staring at her miniature features. It's been so long since my girls were babies, but the wonder and awe of being a new parent floods back like it was yesterday.

"She's beautiful, isn't she?" I ask.

Lexi murmurs in assent.

Little Olive looks straight into my eyes, her mouth tugging into a lopsided smile.

"Thank you for the smile," I whisper. To Lexi, I say, "It's like looking into the eyes of God, isn't it?"

When she doesn't answer, I look up to see her staring at me with a strange look.

"Do you want children?"

Pain flickers across her face, and I want to kick myself in the balls. What in the fuck am I thinking? I've told her there's no possible chance we're having a real relationship, and then I ask her if she wants the full package? What an idiot.

"I used to. I just haven't been...in the right situation to think about it."

I'm an asshole. I have no interest in remarrying or starting a new family. I've been there, done that. No need to do it again.

Although the thought of Lexi's belly swollen with my child does ignite a primal sense of pride.

I pick up the baby and inhale the smell of her, kissing the top of her soft brown curls before handing her back to Joey.

Lexi remains relatively quiet for the rest of the game. I try to tease her out of it, but this problem isn't one I can easily fix for her. Not with money or a little attention.

What she wants, I definitely can't–or am not willing–to give her.

* * *

Lexi

After the game, Bobby drops me off at the apartment without walking me up or coming in for sex.

I can't decide if I'm disappointed or relieved.

It's only been three weeks, and already this situation with Bobby is getting painful. My heart isn't supposed to be involved at all. I wasn't supposed to fall in love. This is a temporary situation. I'd hoped I might stay here a few months to save on rent money and pay down my medical bills. But it's only been a few weeks, and I don't know how much longer I can make it. Every day, I get more and more comfortable. Let him see the real me. Learn to trust him.

But Bobby Manghini isn't available. He's made it clear

I'm not wife-and-kids material. No amount of wishing he would stare at a baby we made together with the same reverence he had at the baseball game would make it happen.

This relationship is purely transactional—he takes care of my financial needs, and I make myself available. Nothing more. Nothing less. The sooner I get back on my feet and can walk away, the better.

I take the elevator up to the apartment and put on a swimsuit. I might as well take advantage of all the luxuries while I'm here. I go up to the rooftop pool. Once again, no one is up there with me. I climb in the pool and float on my back, watching the sky turn pink and purple as the sun sets.

I'm falling in love with a made man. He's wrong for me in so many ways, and yet, I just can't seem to help myself.

Chapter Fourteen

Lexi

The next week, I sit at a hotel conference table across from members of the interview panel.

"Have you ever taught anyone else how to cut or color hair?" the interview panelist asks me, tapping his pen against his teeth.

I expected this question and prepared a dance around it. "I consider myself a mentor to all the other stylists at the salon where I cut. They are always calling me over for a consult, and I'm the one who they trust to cut and color their own hair."

One of the panelists smiles at me. "Who cuts and colors your hair?"

"I do," I admit.

"You don't trust anyone else?"

"Well, not really. Not to do it the way I want it."

The woman smiles and jots something down, but I have a feeling I just scored a point.

"All right, Lexi, now we're going to put your slides up on the big screen, and I'd like you to stand up and explain how you achieved each of these looks and why you chose this design for the client."

I draw in a shaky breath and stand. The photo of Gina appears on the large screen at the front of the room. I walk over. "I chose this look for Gina because of her high cheekbones. I wanted something to highlight, rather than hide them. The jaw-length layers frame her face, and the bold color gives it a bit of spunk, which fits Gina's personality."

I turn to look at the panelists, who appear attentive, if not encouraging. "To achieve this look, I cut the baseline into a diagonal forward and tapered the nape with some graduation. Then I cut some textured, round layers in and over-directed the front to the back layers. For color, I colored the nape area darker and paneled some light and dark color pieces in the front to accentuate the diagonal forward haircut."

I continue through the rest of the slides, gaining confidence as the panelists asked questions I can answer.

"Thank you, Lexi, that will be all for today. If you make it to the next round of interviews, we will ask you to pick one of these looks and teach a sample class to hair stylists. You should hear from us by the end of the week, either way."

"Thank you." I shake hands with each of the panelists before I exit.

When I reach the sidewalk outside, I pull out my phone. The number I call up first belongs to Bobby.

When did he and Gina trade importance in my life?

I shake my head. If I don't watch out, I'll get in too deep with him. He said he'd do anything for me. It seems I share the sentiment. I'd do anything to please him. Things I never dreamed I would let a man do to me. Or *want* a man to do to me.

But I do want it. Every pain he inflicts, every act of dominance only heightens my desire for him.

He picks up after two rings. "How'd it go?" he asks without saying hello.

My heart skips a beat. *He remembered.* Gina would have needed reminding.

"Great! At least I think it went great. It's hard to tell because they just sit and stare at you and make notes on their notepads. But I did as well as I could have. I felt good. I felt confident."

"Congratulations! Are you headed home? Why don't I pick you up there in an hour, and we'll go out to dinner to celebrate?"

My heart tumbles around in my chest. "Sounds great, thanks!"

I take the subway train home and open the door.

I stop short when I see someone inside. It's cleaning day, but they should have been gone by now.

"Oh, great, you're home!"

I stare in shock as Stacy, Bobby's ex-girlfriend, walks toward me with a smile, carrying a half-full glass of wine. She's wearing a tight leather mini-skirt and even smaller top, her breasts practically spilling out of her push-up bra.

"Wh-what are you doing here?"

"Bobby asked me to come. He didn't tell you?"

My stomach tightens. I hate everything about this–especially after what happened last time I talked to her. "Uh, no." I pull my phone out to double-check for a text.

Stacy lowers her lashes and gives me a seductive look. "Yeah, he said he wanted to try a threesome with the two of us. Maybe he wanted it to be a surprise."

I continue to stare blankly at my cell phone as if it would somehow decode the situation. Was that why he arranged to meet me here so early? Not to take me to dinner but for a threesome?

I feel nauseous. I have no interest in a threesome. Especially not with Stacy, whose cheap floozy look and pushy personality turn me off. Maybe if Bobby were here, I would feel differently. He's pushed me sexually in other ways, and I enjoyed it. But God, he should've talked to me about it first! And to say we're celebrating my interview and then pull this surprise instead– none of it sits well with me.

"Mind if I put on some music?" Stacy asks.

"Um...sure. Go ahead."

"I opened a bottle of wine," she calls over her shoulder. "Bobby said we should get the party started before he gets here. Did he say what time he's coming?"

I swallow, trying to push down the growing sense of violation I feel. "He should be here soon," I mutter.

Stacy puts on some dance music and cranks the volume. She dances back, pulling off her top to reveal her breasts stuffed in a bra at least two sizes too small.

"Go get some wine!" Stacy calls out over the music.

I walk to the kitchen, annoyed when I see the state of it. Stacy obviously struggled with the cork, which lies in pieces all over the counter. She spilled wine while pouring it and didn't bother to wipe it up. Pieces of cork float on the top of the wine, so when I pour myself a glass, I have to fish them out.

I take a sip and head back into the living room, knowing I don't want wine or her in my home. Certainly not my bed. But I don't make the rules.

Stacy dances over to me, insinuating her body against mine in a gyration to the beat. "Come on! Bobby said we should get started without him! Imagine how hot it will be for him to find us making out when he gets here!" She puts her hands on the two sides of my face and comes in close for a kiss.

I pull away. I have no interest in this threesome, especially not without Bobby here.

The door opens as Stacy pulls her lips away and Bobby comes in, his brows drawing together.

He frowns and looks confused. "What the fuck?"

Realizing I've been had–*again*–I take a step back from Stacy.

"I came for that threesome we always talked about," she trills.

"She said you arranged it," I tell Bobby, letting him hear the annoyance in my voice.

He closes his eyes like he's trying to draw the patience necessary for handling this. He walks over to the stereo and turns off the music. "Get out." He looks at Stacy and jerks his head toward the door.

"Bob-bee!" Stacy protests. "She's into it. We were having a great time. Come and join in!"

I shoot him a look and shake my head.

Bobby takes a menacing step toward Stacy. "Lexi and I have plans tonight, and they don't include you. Go on, get out."

Stacy drops her act, anger flashing across her overly-made-up face.

"How did you get in, anyway?" I demand, my eyes narrowed. I definitely don't want a repeat of this situation. "Do you still have a key?"

Stacy grins triumphantly. "Cleaning day. The maids still remember me."

Bobby swears softly in Italian. "Stacy." He sounds like he's working to keep his voice level. "It's over. I will *never* pick things up with you again. Now get the fuck out of my apartment." He reaches for her elbow, but she twists out of his grip and darts around behind the sofa with a squeal of delight. "Ooh, I'm misbehaving!" she calls out. "You'd better spank me!"

"*Fanculo*," Bobby mutters. He glowers at her. "Stacy." His voice is deadly. "You don't want to cross me."

She must get the message because she falters, the smile dropping away replaced by anger again. "Oh yeah? What are you going to do? Shoot me? Beat me?" She sends me a wild look. "He likes to hurt women, you know. He abused me."

"Out." Bobby uses icy authority. "I don't want to see you again. I don't want to hear you spoke to Lexi again. You don't come here, and you'd better not show your face at Swank. If you do, I'm going to send my boys over to take back every gift I ever gave you, plus interest, understand?"

She pales. Apparently Bobby's found the best leverage on her: greed.

She looks over at me again. "He'll get tired of you. Just like he got tired of me. Don't get too comfortable in this fancy apartment because it won't last!"

I feel sick, but I lift my chin. "Don't compare yourself to me," I say evenly. "We're nothing alike."

"That's the truth," Bobby says.

Stacy throws her wine glass at me. I dodge it, and it smashes into the wall next to me. One of the shards of glass embeds in my upper arm.

"Fuck you both," Stacy spits, flipping me off.

I wince and pull the triangle of glass out of my arm, which produces a surprising amount of blood.

Bobby turns pale, staring at the blood, and then he snatches Stacy by the throat, pressing her against the wall. "*You hurt her*," he growls.

"Bobby!" I cry out, remembering his story about the bloody nose and the gun. He's not himself. I rush to his side and grab his arm. "Bobby, stop!"

He looks at me, and I don't recognize the man. His eyes are dark and dead, his face is made of stone.

"Bobby, *let her go.*"

He looks back at Stacy then at me.

"*Bobby.* I'm okay."

He blinks, then suddenly he transforms back to the man I know. He releases her abruptly and steps back. "Fuck."

Stacy lurches away, snatches up her top then runs in her platform heels to grab her purse from the kitchen, leaving without another word or backward glance.

When Bobby turns his gaze back to me, his expression is wracked with horror.

* * *

Bobby

Fuck. What have I done?

Contrary to what Stacy asserted, I don't abuse women. At least I haven't until now. I just saw Lexi bleeding, and my brain registered her injury as life-threatening. The urge to eliminate all threats to Lexi's life overcame me.

I didn't mean to manhandle Stacy.

Even now, I'm still in shock. I know I need to work my ass off to fix this situation right now, but I can't seem to make myself move.

"Lexi," I croak.

Unbelievably, she doesn't seem furious. She's not rushing to pack her bags and move out. "It's okay." She takes my arm. "I'm okay, Bobby."

"No, you're not," I manage to say. Blood still streams down her arm, dripping onto the carpet.

The image of my father, bleeding out behind the wheel of his Mercedes as I crouched on the floorboard and pulled his gun from the glove box...fuck.

I thought I was long past this.

Lexi calmly walks to the kitchen, and I finally make myself move to follow. "No, stay out there," she tells me. "I'm going to clean this up, so you don't have to look at it."

My brain barely registers what she's saying. So I...*don't have to look*? Is *she* actually taking care of *me* in this situation?

I'm the fuck-up here.

I move, jerky-limbed, to clean up the glass on the floor. When I bring it into the kitchen, Lexi has cleaned the blood off her arm and is attempting to pry a smaller piece of glass from her flesh.

"Let me, baby. May I?" My voice sounds hoarse.

She nods, and I gently tug her under the light, so I can locate the offending sliver. I want to pull her into my arms but don't dare because I'm not sure where we stand after that dose of crazytown. After what I just did. "I'm so sorry."

I have to blink and control my breath because the sight of her blood seeping around my fingers keeps making me flash to my father. The way the blood poured down the side of his face after his forehead hit the steering wheel. The crunch and scream of metal as the car crashed into the streetlight.

"I'm okay, Bobby. Are you okay?" Her breath is soft on my face. I'm the kinda guy who doesn't like to show weakness, but for some reason, it feels okay that Lexi knows I lost my shit back there. That I'm still losing my shit.

My fingernail scrapes over the shard of glass, and she jerks. "Sorry sweetheart. I've almost got it."

A couple more scrapes, and I manage to extricate the glass. "Got it." I show her the tiny sliver on the pad of my index finger. I'm breathing heavily, like I just finished a workout.

"Thanks."

I swallow. "Lexi...I don't even know what to say. I guess I thought you were in danger, and I just sort of...overreacted."

"Was it the blood?"

I draw in a breath and let it out. "It was...yeah, I think that's what happened." I stab my fingers through my hair. "*Cristo.*" I spread my hands. "I've never touched her like that before. You gotta believe me. I don't hurt women, Lex. I mean–"

"I know." Unbelievably, she wraps her arms around my waist and lays her face against my chest.

I exhale, holding her close, kissing the top of her head. "Those things she said–"

"She's a liar," Lexi interrupts. "I should've kicked her out the moment I got home. I'm just so damn gullible."

"No." I cradle Lexi's face to lift it to mine. "No, baby. You're sweet as fuck. You're kind and agreeable and being rude isn't in your nature."

"I'm so glad you didn't actually invite her here for a threesome."

My upper lip curls. "Is that what she told you?"

"Yeah. So..."

She trails off, but I follow the thread of her thoughts. "And you wanted to please me, so you went along with it."

She shrugs. "Sort of. Yeah... I didn't know what to do."

I pull her roughly against me again. "Sweet as fuck," I

mutter, kissing the top of her head. "How can I make this up to you?"

She lifts that dazzling blue gaze. "Well, I thought you were taking me to dinner."

"I sure as hell am."

She walks to the closet and pulls out a broom and dustpan.

I take it from her and point to the bar stool in front of the breakfast bar. "You sit. Don't move. I'll get you a bandage for that cut, and then I'll clean up the mess." I find an adhesive bandage in the bathroom and return, applying it to her arm, needing to take care of her like I need my next breath.

After I sweep up the remaining broken glass, I dump it in the trash then return with a rag to wipe up the spilled wine.

"Some wine spilled on the rug." Lexi sounds angry.

"It'll come out," I promise. "If it doesn't, I'll replace it, okay, babe? I don't want you to worry about it. This was supposed to be your special night."

Lexi moves to stand, but I point to her. "I said don't move, doll."

She rolls her eyes but smiles.

I find a spray cleaner under the sink and scrub the stain on the rug. It doesn't come out, but I move the coffee table leg over by a few inches, and it covers it.

"I'll buy a new rug, okay?"

She shrugs. "It's not my rug."

"Yeah, but you're the one who has to live with it. And I don't want you thinking about what happened." I put the cleaning supplies away and wash my hands. "Can you do me a favor and just erase it forever from your mind?"

"It's fine, Bobby." She hops off the stool and comes to

me. "It wasn't your fault. I'm not upset." She stands on her tiptoes to kiss me, and I go in hungry, grasping the back of her head to kiss her deeply.

The kiss is different this time. It's not driven by lust although I do want her. I always want her. No, this is more of an expression of...fuck. An expression of love.

I'm in deep with Lexi now.

Something tells me it's time to reevaluate our situation.

Then again, it's working. If we need to adjust later, we can.

Chapter Fifteen

Lexi

On Friday afternoon, I finally get the call about the job. I've been waiting all week for the news. Bobby was over every night in time for dinner, which helped the time go by. He brought flowers and wine. Bags of specialty groceries–expensive stuff that I wouldn't buy for myself. I loved cooking for him. He's so easy to please.

He took me to dinner a couple of times, and we stayed in watching a movie one night.

For someone who's not supposed to be my boyfriend, he sure as hell acts like one. Another great thing about this past week is that for the first time in a long time, my earnings belong to me. Well, not really, because I still have the thirty thousand in medical bills to pay off, but there's no looming financial emergency. I'm making enough this month to pay the rent at the salon, put some toward the medical bills, and still be able to buy lunch at the deli.

"This is Lexi," I answer breathlessly, recognizing the phone number.

"Hi Lexi, this is Erica Applegate, Human Resources Director at Stellar.

"Yes, hi!"

"I just wanted to let you know that you made it to the next round. The next step is for you to teach a sample class to a group of stylists. Does next Thursday at eleven work for you?"

I hold the phone away from my face and silently fist-pump in the air. When I come back, I attempt to sound calm and collected. "That's great. Yes, I can rearrange my schedule for that time."

"Great, I'll email you the interview confirmation with the details. We'll see you next week."

I hang up and catch Ondrea craning her head from the reception desk to meet my gaze. She's the only one at Stylz who knows about this job, and until I land it, that's the way it's going to stay. I told her in confidence that I'd made it to the interview round and was waiting for the call. I give her the thumbs up, and she mimes a silent scream of joy back.

Smiling, I turn back to my station.

Bobby texted earlier to say he was tied up tonight, so after work, I head to Swank to celebrate with Gina.

When I push open the door, I find myself praying Stacy won't be there.

He'll get tired of you. Just like he got tired of me.

I can't get her words out of my mind. Bobby was sweet that night, treating me to a fancy dinner and doting on me—and I assured him I wasn't upset. I know he assumed I was horrified that he'd choked her. And I was—a little.

But I was also a tiny bit gratified. His instinct had been to protect me. From her.

That has to mean I'm more than his usual floozie, right?

I really, really want to believe that's true. I want to be more to him. I want to be...everything.

But the reality is that I could be another Stacy tomorrow.

Aw, fuck. I spot the blonde sitting at the bar when I walk in. She clearly didn't follow his order not to come here. I hesitate in the doorway. Maybe I should just go home. I can always call Gina.

No, screw that. I straighten my shoulders. I've been coming to this club for years, and I'm not going to be scared off by some psycho ex-girlfriend. I march over to the end of the bar and wait for Gina to see me. The Friday happy hour crowd packs the place, the young professionals looking smart in their suits. I catch sight of a tall, broad-shouldered man, and my heart stops for a moment, thinking it's Bobby. But that's stupid. He has me at his beck and call. Why would he be out trolling for someone else?

"Hey, girl!" Gina slaps a cocktail napkin down in front of me. "What are you drinking?"

"Lemon Drop, please."

"Have you heard anything about the job?"

I hold both arms up in the air and roll my hips in a victory dance. "Guess who made the next round, uh huh, that's right."

"Yeah, you did! I knew it. That's so great." Gina fills a martini glass with ice to chill while she fills her stainless steel mixing container with Smirnoff vodka, Cointreau, lemon juice, syrup and ice. She gives it a good shake before pouring the liquid through the strainer into the chilled glass.

"Now I give a sample class and teach a group of stylists how to do a hairstyle."

"Nice."

"So did Bobby's ex-girlfriend say anything to you? About me? Or Bobby?"

"No, why?" Gina leans her forearms on the bar with interest.

I fill her in on the drama that went down at the apartment.

"Holy shit," Gina said. "Well, if she gives you any trouble, let me know, and I'll have Leo throw her out."

"Thanks. Bobby did tell her not to come here again. You know, I have to say, part of me wanted him to go totally mafia on her ass." I laugh. "You know, like tell her if she showed up again, she would be swimming with the fishes."

Gina laughs. "I don't blame you."

"But I guess the fact that he was appropriately disturbed by his own violence is a good sign. You know, in case I'm ever the one he's mad at."

Gina snorts. "In case you turn into stalker girl?"

"No. But I've been a little wary. Because of the mafia thing. He's always been a gentleman, but I guess I had this worry in the back of my mind that I'd better not seriously piss him off, or I'd be in actual, mortal danger."

"Well," Gina muses. "You'd probably have to do something really terrible for that to happen. Like wear a wire or steal enormous sums of money from him. And you'd never do something like that."

"Right." I glance across the bar to where Stacy sits. "Oh shit, she sees me."

"I'm staying right here with you," Gina says.

Stacy slides off her bar stool and makes her way over. "Hi." She flips her hair back over her shoulder.

I assess her coolly. "I did not appreciate your little stunt this week. I have nothing to say to you."

"Where's your loverboy? Out looking for fresh meat?"

Gina straightens. "Bobby told you not to come here again." She motions to Leo, who walks over, looking aggressive.

Stacy's eyes narrow. "I gave you a chance. We could've shared him."

"Not happening," I tell her.

When Leo arrives, Gina says, "Leo, she's eighty-sixed."

"Let's go," Leo barks.

"Well, I'm not worried," Stacy says to me, ignoring Leo. "He'll get tired of you soon." She tosses her hair again and flounces out of the bar, with Leo walking behind to make sure she really leaves.

"Um..." Gina says. "I hope she's not as psycho as she seems. Maybe he *should* have told her she was going to swim with the fishes."

I force a laugh.

Damn Bobby for choosing such a loser, anyway. And how many more women like her did he have in his past?

Chapter Sixteen

Bobby

obby
For the first time in, well, *ever*, I wish I brought a date to a family event.

We're at my cousin Mario's wedding Friday evening, but being here with the twins feels wrong. I don't mean that it was wrong to bring them, but it feels like something's missing.

Lexi's missing.

But I couldn't bring her here. You can't enmesh outsiders with the Family. It was sticky enough to get divorced. I got grilled a hundred times by Al about how much my ex knew and what kind of liability she'd be. No one wanted me to cut her loose. Divorce is uncommon in *La Cosa Nostra*. The only way out of The Family is in a box, as they say.

But as I sit and watch the young people dancing on the ballroom floor, I wish I was out there, holding Lexi's perfect curves up against my body. I'm sure she's a great dancer. And she *would* fit in here. She's the type who can make conversation with anyone. The family would love her, except for those who say I'm robbing the cradle.

The music changes to a slow song, and I watch Carlo glance at the don before he makes his way to Summer's side. Dangerous territory for him. He should stop pining for the don's daughter before he gets himself in more trouble than he can handle.

Summer lights up when he takes her hand, though, and I have to admit, the two make a beautiful couple.

Janine and Juliana spin off the dance floor and plop down at our table.

"Summer gets all the hot guys," Janine mutters to her sister.

"Seriously. I want Carlo. He has the sexiest accent."

My brain implodes at everything that's wrong about what I just overheard.

"Dad's stroking out right now." Janine laughs.

"Maybe now is the right time to mention I have a date tomorrow," Juliana says brightly. "With a guy from school."

I loosen my tie. Force my fingers to unflex. I want to be cool here. It's better if I know what's going on in their lives than if they hide things from me.

"Is he picking you up at the house?"

"Are you kidding? No chance. I'm not going to let you intimidate him. I like this guy."

I nod. "Fine. If you won't let me meet him, pass along a message from me. You just tell him I will break both his arms if he hurts you."

"That would be funny if it weren't true," Janine observes. "And speaking of introductions. Why didn't you bring Lexi to the wedding?"

"Yeah, Dad. You look lonely," Juliana chimes in.

"I'm not lonely." I frown to shut them up, but they're already on a roll.

"When do we get to meet her?" Janine asks.

"I already told you we're not doing that." Although the idea of introducing them actually does appeal to me. The girls would probably like her if they could get over the fact that she's only seven years older than they are. Lexi would like them, I'm sure. She's the type who makes friends easily. It's worth considering for the future.

I stand when Jessie and Dean walk by. The girls crowd in to ogle baby Olive.

"Oh my God, she's the cutest baby ever. Can I hold her?" Juliana gives Olive an exaggerated smile as she reaches for her.

"Where is Lexi?" Jessie asks.

Janine gives an exaggerated gasp and turns to me, her jaw open. "Jessie's met Lexi, and we haven't?" she demands.

I roll my eyes. "We went to a Yankees game together. It wasn't planned."

Janine shakes her head and looks to Dean and Jessie for support. "I don't get it. Is there something wrong with her? Why won't you bring her around?"

"No, she's great," Jessie says. "He's probably just trying to keep things uncomplicated."

I shake my head and walk off before they can razz me any further. I need a drink.

I find Al at the bar with Joey. "Why aren't you out there dancing?" I ask Joey after ordering a Glenlivit on the rocks. He's usually quick to spin a woman around the floor for a dance.

He grimaces. "I strained my back lifting weights yesterday."

"You're getting old." Al sips a glass of grappa.

"That's you." Joey is fifteen years younger than Al–they're half brothers.

"You should go get a massage. I heard Artie Palazzo's daughter is a masseuse now. You should see her. It'd be good to throw her some cash, you know?" Al reminds Joey of Artie Palazzo, a made man who was killed years ago. The Family takes care of their own in a case like that, and we had, but his widow and daughter Sophie had worked to put distance between themselves and La Cosa Nostra in the years since.

"So what's the word with the Feds?" Al asks, but his gaze is on Carlo and Summer. As if Carlo senses it, the moment the song ends, he gives Summer a polite kiss on the cheek and makes his way to us.

"Crawling up my ass."

"They gonna find anything?"

I shake my head. "Nope. But they're costing me in headaches. Plus, I'll have to triple future payoffs to the mayor after this."

"That sucks." Al watches Carlo approach with a stony expression.

I shrug. "It's no big deal. Chalk it up to the cost of doing business. I'm satisfied knowing they're pouring their resources into a fruitless investigation."

Al snorts. "Right. Thank you for that."

"Anytime, Boss."

Carlo orders a drink and leans an elbow on the bar near us.

"Who do you think talked?" Al asks. I catch the danger in his gaze. Informers are eliminated. Immediately.

I shake my head. "No one on my side. I'm careful as fuck. Greta knows nothing, and she's family, anyway." My secretary is the sister of one of the soldiers in the organization.

"What about your girlfriends? That stripper who was getting pushy? Any of them know anything?"

My pulse speeds up. Stacy was a pain in my ass, but that doesn't mean I want her in the don's crosshairs. And just *the idea* of him threatening Lexi makes me itchy and hot.

"They're clean. No contact to my business. Ever."

"What about contact to your phone?"

"No." Somehow I manage to keep my gaze perfectly steady despite the twitch of my fingers to close into a fist. Lexi had my phone the one time, but I believed her that it was a mistake. She saw a text about the investigation. Nothing damning. Nothing she could testify about.

Al's eyes narrow like he knows I'm lying. "You sure about that?" There's a thread of menace in his voice.

I'm not gonna come clean. Not to throw Lexi under a bus.

So I just nod my head. "Yeah. I'm sure. One hundred percent."

* * *

Lexi

I text Bobby's number the minute I walk out of the sample class Friday evening. *I just taught my class!*

And? he replies ten minutes later.

I think I rocked it. I send him a fingers crossed emoji.

You got this, he replies. *I'm tied up tonight, but I'll try to get over there by 9.*

I try to swallow my disappointment. I'd been hoping for another fancy dinner to celebrate. I'm getting spoiled.

Okay, see you then, I text back.

At 8:30 p.m., I take a bath in the big jacuzzi tub and put on a lacy bralette and matching lacy panties. When 9 p.m. rolls around, Bobby doesn't show or text.

At 9:30 p.m. I get a text saying, *Running late.*

I send back the simple one-letter reply, *K,* expecting he meant a few more minutes late. By 10 p.m., though, I'm getting antsy.

I guess I'm addicted to Bobby. Or his orgasms. Or something. I need satisfaction, and only he can bring it.

What's up? I text.

Sorry, baby, I'm still tied up but definitely coming. Be there in less than an hour.

At 11 p.m., when he still hasn't arrived, I text, *WTF?*

He doesn't reply.

Still not ready to throw in the towel and go to bed, I keep my sexy outfit on and sit on the sofa, watching TV. I've mostly written him off but still feel like I should wait up to see if he ever responds.

Twenty minutes later he walks through the door looking like he just stepped off the cover of a men's magazine. He's in an expensive suit and tie, but he smells faintly of whiskey. His eyes glitter with dark purpose.

"What is this?" He raises a brow and shows me the screen of his phone, which displays my last text message.

"Oops." Yeah, I'm guessing the mob boss doesn't like disrespectful texts. Note to self–don't brat the guy who gets off on delivering punishment.

Or maybe I should. Because I can tell he's relishing the idea of punishing me.

The clenching between my legs tells me I'm relishing it, too.

His lips twitch like he thinks I'm cute. He shrugs out of his jacket. "Yeah. Oops. Someone's in trouble now."

I stand and walk around the sofa to greet him. "Sorry?"

He tosses jacket and phone onto the glass coffee table. He unbuttons the cuff of one sleeve and starts to roll it up. "I understand I disrespected your time, but we do have an agreement: you are available to me. Not the other way around."

I hold his gaze and lower to my knees, unbuckling his belt and opening his trousers.

He goes still when I release his erection, as if he can't roll up the other cuff while I'm touching him there. "That would be a nice apology, *bambina*."

I fist the base of his cock and moisten my lips before I slide them slowly over the head.

He groans and rolls up the other cuff. He's making a show of it for my benefit, I'm sure.

I do my best to make it up to him, taking him deep into the pocket of my cheek then coming off to let the air cool his skin before I take him deep again. He groans. "That's it, *bambina*."

I love his approval. I continue to work his cock, sometimes concentrating on the head, then taking him straight to the back of my throat, relaxing my gag reflex to take him all the way.

He mutters a curse in Italian and fists my hair in the back. I love the roughness, especially when he starts controlling my head, pulling me on and off, then holding me still, so he can shove in and out.

He comes in my mouth, and I suck him clean, drinking in the warmth of his gaze as he puts his cock away. "That was nice, but it doesn't get you out of your punishment." He smirks and sits down on the couch, then pats his thighs. "Come here, baby."

My stomach flutters as I obey his command, kneeling beside him to drape myself over his lap.

He starts spanking with his hand, one cheek, then the other, then square in the middle. I squirm as the fire begins to set in.

He pauses and pulls my lacy panties down. They catch underneath me, and tear. "Oops. Sorry, baby. I'll buy you new ones."

He strokes my bare skin, making goosebumps rise before he begins to spank again. I squeeze my cheeks together and straighten my legs, stiffening like a surfboard.

"Push your ass out," he commands.

I don't move for a moment, and he doesn't resume, clearly waiting for me to follow his instructions. I consider ignoring them, but of course, it would get me nowhere. I'm the one folded over his lap with my panties down. I release my clenched butt muscles and hollow my back, presenting my butt for his punishment.

"Good girl." He begins to spank again, methodically, evenly, one side then the other, right on the place where cheek meets thigh.

I wriggle over his lap.

"I'm sorry!" I gasp when it starts to burn, reaching back to try to cover my butt. Bobby takes my wrist and bends my arm behind my back, pinning it there while he continues to apply rapid-fire smacks to the lower half of my ass. To my surprise, he shifts the grasp on my wrist so he's holding my hand instead, as if offering tenderness or support while he inflicts pain.

The endorphins kick in. A rush of pleasure at the pain

soaks through me, along with an ocean of affection for my punisher.

"I'm sorry!" I repeat.

"Sorry for what?" He traces a circle around my ass, soothing away the sting.

"Sorry for pissing you off?"

He chuckles. "Wrong answer." He gives me two more spanks. "Sorry for pissing me off means you don't think you did anything wrong."

"I'm sorry I cursed?" I keep groping. "Sorry I disrespected you."

Bobby's hand tangles in my hair in an unhurried caress. He delivers several more spanks, then dips his fingers between my legs and rubs over my soaked slit. "Mmm. You liked your spanking," he rumbles, obviously enjoying himself.

I wiggle my ass on his lap. I'm ready for more–pain or pleasure–whatever he wants to deliver. I want it all.

The intensity of this relationship matches no other. With Bobby, I've been my most vulnerable and found in him more concern, attention and caring than I've ever received from any man. He handles intimacy better than anyone I know—hell, he demands it from me. And he proves himself worthy of it, again and again.

He finds my clit and circles it and a mini-orgasm ripples through me. "That's right, baby," he murmurs. "I like when you come on my fingers."

Bobby lifts me to straddle his lap. I wrap my arms around his neck and rock over the bulge in his pants. "You're not really mad at me, are you?" I ask, even though I already know he's enjoying himself thoroughly.

"Mad *about* you," he murmurs in my hair. He kisses me, then pulls away, and strokes my lower lip with his thumb.

I take it into my mouth and suck. Hard.

His gaze darkens. He pats the sofa cushion. "Kneel up, *bambi*."

I climb onto my knees facing the back of the couch. Bobby stands behind me and rolls on a condom. I'm already in outer space, so the moment he pushes into me, my eyes roll back in my head with pleasure. He grips my hips and fucks me roughly, his loins slapping against mine. I put my hands onto the back of the couch, bracing myself, pushing my ass back to take him even deeper.

The room swoops and tilts like I'm on a rollercoaster. I'm lightheaded, awash with pleasure. Bobby's fingers tighten around my hips, his thrusts grow more rough.

"Please," I whimper, needing to come again.

"Wait for permission," he growls.

I hold my breath, holding off the orgasm hurtling closer as he continues to slam into me.

"Now, baby." His voice chokes as he shoves in deep and spends. He reaches around to the front of my hips and rubs over my clit, and I shatter, ecstasy exploding from my core outward in spirals of heat and endorphins.

My shriek echoes off the walls, my toes curl. I shake and shudder and wring out every last drop of pleasure from Bobby's cock.

Bobby continues to lightly stroke my clit. "And that's what happens when you're a bad girl," he rumbles with satisfaction.

Chapter Seventeen

Bobby

I study Lexi as she sleeps. I spent the night with her. I told myself it was because it was too late to go home, but the truth was that I didn't want to leave.

Sleeping apart from Lexi is starting to feel wrong.

I texted Juliana and Janine last night to let them know I wouldn't be home.

Now I lean up on one elbow to take in her beautiful face in the morning light. Her thick shiny hair fans out across her pillow, her lashes are long and dark against delicate skin. She has the sort of beauty that would last into old age—fine bone structure, big eyes and a generous smile.

I resist the urge to caress her face, not wanting to wake her.

Her lashes flutter open, and she stares at me, her lips stretching into a wide smile. "You stayed." She throws a leg over mine and grinds her mons against it.

Her sex drive is incredible.

She slides her hand over my chest, resuming a slow undulation with her pelvis. "You're the boss."

I laugh, picking up the cue. "That's right, little girl."

The juices from her pussy dampen my leg. She gets up to her hands and knees and crawls down over me. "May I suck your dick?"

My cock, already standing at attention, surges with delight. "Please."

She opens her mouth, swirling her tongue over the head of my dick. She lifts her eyes to mine at the moment she takes my full length into her mouth, making me shudder with pleasure.

"Lexi..." I mutter, my voice thick.

"Mmm hmm?" she hums, sliding my cock into the pocket of her cheek then down the back of her throat.

"You give the best head." I burrow my fingers into her silky hair and massage her scalp. "But you already know that, don't you, sweetheart?"

She hums again and begins to work her hands in a twisting motion at the base of my cock, dragging one up toward the head while the other grips the base in a tight squeeze.

"That apology blowjob you gave me last night was so hot. I love it when you get on your knees for me."

She quickens her pace as if turned on by my praise.

I groan. As she bobs up and down over my cock, I start to come apart, fisting her hair to control her head. I move her up and down until I pull her off, shouting, "*God, yes!*" as I come.

Not wanting to make Lexi wait to get off, I grab her and pull her down beside me, spreading her thighs to return the favor. I lick into her, swirling my tongue around her clit, sucking the little nub, using my fingers to plunge inside.

Lexi lies back, making encouraging noises but not really getting anywhere.

"Do you ever come when someone licks your pussy, Lexi?"

She shakes her head. "No...I mean, it's great! It feels good, but..."

I remember our first night, at Swank, when she seemed doubtful I could get her off. I crawl over her. "How about missionary style? Do you ever orgasm in that position?"

Again she shakes her head, then shrugs. "I never have, but maybe with you."

I smile, honored by her confidence in my abilities. "All right, I'll take that challenge."

I crawl off the bed and open a dresser drawer, pulling out one of her bras.

"What are you doing?"

I slide the arm loop of her bra over one of the posts of the bed, then grab her wrists and pin them over her head, knotting the bra around them.

"Ooh," she squeals. "I'm not sure it counts as missionary if my hands are bound."

Hoisting her legs into the air, I hold her ankles with one hand and gave her ass a slap. "Who's running this show, *bambi*?"

She gives a husky laugh. "You are. Master."

I lower her hips, running my thumb along her glossy slit. "Good girl. I make the rules here. You lie back and take it. And right now, you're going to take it in missionary position."

She bucks even more at my fondling, or maybe my words, her hips bobbing under my thumb.

I ease her feet back to the bed. "Open your knees, *bambina*."

She bends her knees with her feet wide apart and arches her pelvis in my direction.

"Oh, now you're begging for it, aren't you?" I give her pussy a light slap.

She cries out but doesn't close her legs, just pants, watching me with excitement.

"You're going to want to come the second my cock penetrates that pretty little pussy of yours, but you can't. Not until I say you can." I slap her pussy again. "Understand, beautiful?"

"Yes, sir!"

"Good girl." I roll on a condom and shove into her, deep enough to make her moan. "That's right," I murmur, sliding out and repeating the aggressive plunge. "I'm going to fuck you so hard you'll never forget who owns you."

She moans, arching up, her eyelashes fluttering.

I plumb her depths, lowering my head to one nipple, teasing it with my tongue then nipping with my teeth. I give it a light slap which makes her pussy gush, her hips gyrating in a frantic rhythm beneath me.

I stay with that rhythm, letting her rock her clit against me on each in-stroke until her cries become desperate.

"Do you want to come now, Lexi?" I ask, spanking her breast again. "Do you?"

"Yesssss. God, yes!" she cries.

I grip her shoulders, bracing her as I slam inside her over and over again until my own orgasm crests. "Now, Lexi!" I shout when I reach climax.

She goes wild beneath me, wriggling and coming with a cry and a shudder.

"I think," I muse, freeing her wrists as she recovers beneath me, "You just need it rough."

"I think I just need you," she says.

My heart lurches.

She blushes, as if realizing she's shown me all her cards.

I want to tell her I need her too, but it's not my style. I settle for expressing the depth of my emotion for her with the most tender kiss, holding her eyes, so she knows my need.

Chapter Eighteen

Lexi

I float through the next day at work.

I love the way Bobby demands my submission then rewards me thoroughly for giving it. For a natural pleaser like me, it's a win-win. I can't really lose because he tells me exactly what he wants. There's no denying the appeal of a man so clearly in charge of me and the world around him. Or maybe it's as he says–I just need it a little rough.

In the afternoon, a courier delivers a box to Stylz with a dozen pairs of expensive panties from Victoria's Secret. The note reads,

Sorry about ripping your panties last night. Hope these make up for it. Can't wait to see you again.

They're exactly my size and the style I wear.

The day gets even better when I check my phone and find an email came in from Stellar's human resources. I open it and scan the words, hardly able to process what I'm reading: I got the job.

I got the job.

"Hey, Lex?" Ondrea interrupts my reverie. "You have walk-ins requesting you. Can you fit them in?"

"Them?" I glance toward the waiting area where two beautiful young women stand. Sisters–no, twins.

"Well, just one of them wants a cut. But they came in together."

"Sure, I can squeeze her in. Let me just finish cleaning up from the last client."

Ondrea leaves, and I clean up my station, then usher the young women back. One of them plunks down in her seat, and the other sits in the hood dryer seat beside my station to watch.

"Just a trim," the pretty brunette says.

"Keep the layers? Just the way it is?" The young woman doesn't appear to need a cut, but I'm not going to argue. Money is money.

"Yes, please."

"Okay, come on back for a shampoo." I wrap a towel around her neck, clip it in place then lead her back to the sinks to wash and condition her hair.

When we return to my station, she meets my eye in the mirror with an impish look. "You don't know who we are, do you?"

I frown, looking from one face in the mirror, to the identical one sitting nearby.

"Should I?"

"I'm Juliana Manghini, and this is my sister, Janine."

"Oh!" My heartbeat speeds up.

"Bobby is our dad. He didn't tell you about us?"

I take a breath and will myself to speak. "Uh, n-no. I mean, I knew he had kids, but I didn't know the specifics."

I don't know why I feel assaulted by this visit. They seem friendly enough. It doesn't seem like they're here to hate on me. But I knew nothing about them. Not that he had twins. Not that they're grown-ups, not children.

It makes me realize how little I know about my benefactor. Because that's all he is. We're not in a real relationship. Even though that's what I want. Everything is on his terms.

I draw in a breath and force myself to smile. "It's nice to meet you."

The girls smirk, as if they're pleased with themselves for finding me. "Um, how did you find me?"

"Our Aunt Jessie gave me your card at the wedding last night."

Wedding. Last night. That's why he was late.

He was at a wedding. A family wedding that I knew nothing about. My stomach twists. Nothing about this is sitting right with me.

"Technically, she's a cousin," Janine corrects her.

"Right. Whatever. She said she met you at a Yankees game?"

"Uh...yeah," I manage. My hands thankfully operate on their own accord, combing Juliana's hair and parting out sections to trim. "So...why are you here?"

I brace myself, ready for anything. For them to tell me he's married. Or drop some other bomb. Maybe they're trying to expose me as a money-grubbing prostitute. I don't know.

That's definitely how I feel right now.

This thing with Bobby is just a business arrangement. I'm not good enough to take to weddings. Or to introduce to his kids. I'm not worth making a commitment to.

Hell, I'm not even supposed to call his phone. I have to text.

"We just wanted to meet you. He's all secretive about

you. He wasn't going to introduce us, so we figured we'd take it out of his hands."

I'm all awash with cold now. "Oh." That's all I can think to say.

His daughters seem nice. If I'd met them under different circumstances, I'm sure I'd love them. But everything about this interaction is making me dizzy.

Nauseous.

Suddenly, everything I loved about last night seems icky now. He wasn't working late or doing mysterious mafia business. He was at a family wedding. One that I wasn't deemed worthy of attending.

It's not okay.

This situation is no longer okay. Not in the slightest.

I press my lips together, my hands still working steadily, snipping the ends of Juliana's layers.

The sisters exchange another glance and an uncomfortable silence falls. "Sorry if this is weird," Janine says.

"Um, no," I say in a tone of voice that's clearly too high and therefore a lie. "I'm just, ah, realizing that maybe his keeping me a secret doesn't work for me anymore."

Bobby's daughters exchange another look. "Well, don't take it the wrong way. He just doesn't like to mix his dating life with us," Juliana offers. "It's our fault—when our parents first got divorced, we pitched a fit about them dating anyone else."

I force myself to nod, like I understand. Like this all makes perfect sense, when in fact, it's all bullshit. Somehow, I finish the haircut, pick up the blow dryer and turn it on, thankful it drowns out any further attempts at conversation.

When I turn it off, Juliana launches in, as if she's been waiting to speak. "He really likes you, you know. You're the first woman we've heard about. That's why we came to check you out."

My heart constricts. I almost believe her.

But it doesn't matter whether he likes me or not.

He doesn't like me enough.

I can't bring myself to answer. I just force a wan smile as I remove the cape and dust the stray hairs off her neck. "That will be fifty," I manage to say.

She pays me, and they both hesitate, as if wanting to say more, but I turn my back, walking away to fetch the broom. When I return, they're gone.

I sit, trembling.

Bobby's been treating me like a second-class citizen. And for what? To have a laugh at my expense? To keep me at arm's length? Am I not good enough to be an actual girlfriend? Do you have to be Italian to make that cut? Or...what?

I can hardly think, and my next client will be here any minute.

I pick up my phone and hold it with trembling fingers. Thirty minutes ago, I'd been excited to text him to tell him I got the job. Now, though?

I grit my teeth and dial his phone number. I'm not supposed to call, but I don't really care. Or actually, I do care. This is a test.

How he responds will tell me everything.

He doesn't answer.

I Google-search his company and dial that number because he said he had to work today, even though it's a Saturday.

"Lexi, you can't call me here." That's how he answers.

I nod. The invisible guillotine blade just came down on

his neck. "That's what I thought," I say tightly and end the call.

Fuck. Him.

I'm done.

This no longer works for me.

I take care of my next client then slip into the back room to call Gina. I'm afraid I might cry, and I don't want anyone at the salon to see me.

My friend picks up on the second ring. "Hi, Lex." She sounds sleepy, even though it's two in the afternoon. With Gina working late nights and having a hot boyfriend who can't get enough, she often sleeps past noon.

"Sorry did I wake you?"

"Mmm, no. I was just getting up. How are you?"

"Crappy." My voice breaks.

"What happened?"

"I don't know. Bobby's daughters just showed up here to meet me. I guess there was a family wedding yesterday?"

Gina waits.

"Apparently I'm not good enough to merit an invite. Or to even know about it. According to them, he isn't planning on letting them meet me, so they played detective to find me on their own."

"Okay," Gina says slowly like she's trying to understand.

"This isn't working for me. I don't want to just be the whore he keeps for good times."

"Yeah, of course not. But I don't know if it's really like that. Why don't you just talk to him and ask him WTF?"

I make an impatient noise in my throat. "I don't even want to talk to him again. Listen, I'd better go, I have another client coming. Thanks for listening."

"You're welcome. Hey, Lexi?"

"Yeah?"

"Don't feel like you can't leave him because you don't have a place to go. You're still welcome on my couch."

"Thanks," I say heavily. "I appreciate it."

Sleeping on Gina's couch is better than hanging around and being Bobby's plaything.

* * *

Bobby

I was in the middle of another conversation with the damn IRS auditor when Lexi called.

I didn't mean to be a *stronzo*, but I know I offended her. I don't know why she called here, though.

We have boundaries in place. She's not supposed to call me.

Still, I have an uneasy feeling about it all afternoon. I text her back that I'm tied up, but she doesn't reply.

When the IRS auditor finally leaves, I try calling, but she doesn't pick up, so I drive over to the apartment. She was supposed to hear about the job today. Fuck, I hope it wasn't bad news. Maybe that's why she called me at work.

The moment I walk in the apartment, I know something's seriously wrong. The place is spotless. Lexi's normally neat, but it smells like it's been freshly cleaned, and today wasn't a cleaning day.

I find her in the bathroom, scrubbing the tub. She glances up when I walk in and greet her, but she says nothing.

Alarm bells clang in my head.

"Lex? What's going on?"

She just shakes her head and continues to clean. Okay,

so she's one of those people who cleans when she's upset. Got it.

I walk up behind her. "What is it, baby? Did you hear about the job?"

"I got it," she says flatly. She stands and pulls off her rubber gloves, passing me without looking my way.

"That's great." I pause when she continues to avoid eye contact, washing her hands in the sink. "What's going on? Talk to me, *bambina*." I reach for her.

"*Don't.*"

I freeze, yanking my hand back like I'm burnt. For all my aggressive play, I would never handle a woman who doesn't want me, especially not Lexi, whom I genuinely care about.

"What is it?"

She finally turns and looks at me for the first time. "Your daughters came by to tell me about the wedding." Accusation rings in her tone. I take in her expression. There's anger mixed with resolve.

Fuck.

"You're upset."

"No, Bobby. I'm not upset. I'm just done. This doesn't work for me."

I scrub a hand across my face. "You're mad I didn't take you to the wedding? Is that it? I...maybe I should have." I stab my fingers through my hair. *Fanculo*. "Let's talk this over."

She shakes her. "It's okay. I understand. This is an arrangement. You made it perfectly clear you're not my boyfriend. Of course, you wouldn't take me to a family wedding. I get it."

"No." I hold out my palms. "It's not like that. I found myself wishing you were there, doll. I just like to keep things separate for your safety. And because I prefer not to mix my dating life with my kids."

"Your *kids* are nineteen years old!"

"It's just easier this way."

"I know." She brushes past me and walks into the bedroom.

I follow.

"You want someone you can control. Someone you don't have to answer to. You like to play your little games with me, don't you?"

Dammit. This has gone so far off the rails I'm not sure I can recover. She was so agreeable all along. I thought–stupidly–this arrangement was working for her.

"I'm sorry you're upset."

"I'm sorry you're upset means you don't think you did anything wrong." She throws my words back at me.

She's right.

But am I truly sorry? Not really. I liked our arrangement. I don't want the boring, vanilla sort of dating life a girlfriend would entail.

"Lex," I coax. "I didn't mean to hurt you. It's just the way I wanted our relationship to go. You seemed perfectly happy to accept it, so I didn't see a problem."

Tears fill her eyes, but judging from the set of her jaw, they're the angry kind. "I just need some time to think. Could you leave? I want you to go."

My heart twists painfully in my chest.

A tear slides down her cheek.

It takes everything in my power not to lunge forward and fold her up into my arms. But she doesn't want to be touched. Not by me. Not now, anyway.

"Lexi," I try again.

"Please," she begs. "Please? Just go?"

Coldness descends from my heart all the way to my shoes. "Yeah, okay," I say. "We'll talk in the morning, okay?"

She needs space, so I'll give it to her.

She doesn't answer–not that I expected her to.

I walk out, turning my mind off.

I don't want to think about how I fucked this up. Badly.

Maybe irreparably.

I hate leaving things unresolved between us. It goes against all my better instincts. I should stay and fight for her. But I respect her too much to ignore her wishes.

I just hope I can come up with the right words tomorrow to make her stay.

* * *

Lexi

I lied to Bobby.

I don't need space. I need to get out of here.

After he leaves, I pack my things. I don't have anywhere to put my furniture and the stuff that's in storage in the basement of the building, but I can worry about that later.

I have a new job now with a guaranteed salary. I can buy myself new things when I get my own place.

Right now, I just need to get out of this apartment. As far away from all the things that remind me of Bobby as I can.

I'm not angry. I mean I am, but I have no right to be. Bobby was up front with me from the start about the parameters of our relationship. I'm the fool who had to want more.

The fool who fell in love.

I could stay. Enjoy his luxury apartment and the great

sex. But every day I stayed would chip away more and more at my dignity. Eat holes through my heart.

No, it's better to just cut my losses now before I get even more attached.

It takes me until midnight, but I get everything I own neatly packed up and ready to go, and then I call a taxi to take me first to Swank to get the key and then to Gina's place.

When I get there, it takes me ninety minutes to move my stuff inside, shower, and curl up on the couch.

I want to cry, but I don't even have the energy.

I'm too drained to even absorb how much grief I carry in my body. In my soul.

I'm too exhausted to even know how much burning this bridge will ultimately cost me.

Chapter Nineteen

Bobby

B I spend a restless night, dreaming of being interrogated by the Feds, who somehow have Lexi standing behind them, her arms folded as if they're working for her.

Last night, I drove home, trying to ignore the sick feeling in my stomach, the cold circling through my veins. I picked up the phone a dozen times to call Lexi then hit "end" before it rang. What would I say that I hadn't already said? I don't know how to change her perception of what had happened.

When I wake in the morning, I check my phone to see if she's called. She hasn't, but of course, I have three messages from the fucking mayor about the investigation on his phone. I cannot even begin to deal with his petulance at this moment.

I skip calling her, opting to drive over as soon as I shower, a pressing sense of urgency moving me forward.

As soon as I get there, I know: she's gone.

Fuck.

I should never have walked out. I should have stayed and figured out the right thing to say to make her stay.

The phone I gave her lies on the table, along with the keys to the apartment. I jog into the bedroom. Everything's gone. No clothes, no boxes. Nothing in the bathroom.

Fanculo.

I punch the wall, the plaster caving under my knuckles.

I try her number on my phone, but, of course, she doesn't answer.

I take the elevator to the basement to check the storage area. Her furniture's still packed in the storage area where my guys moved it. At least I have this small connection to her. She'll have to contact me to get her things. The glimmer of satisfaction doesn't even come close to burning away the ice cold that's filtered through my body. I need to track her down long before she comes for her furniture. I need to find her and fix this.

The trouble is, I have a terrible feeling it's already too late.

* * *

Lexi

I wake with a crick in my neck from sleeping on Gina's couch and an ache in my chest that won't go away.

I try to tell myself I made the right choice.

I couldn't stay with Bobby. If I saw him again, I'd fall for his charisma and that powerful personality. Even when I asked him to leave, I half hoped he'd refuse—maybe chain me to the bed. Give me orgasms until I lose my mind and agree to stay.

Don't Tease Me

I get up and wash my face, being quiet so I won't wake Gina and Leo, who returned home from work at three a.m.

I skip breakfast, too tied up in knots to get anything down. I search for apartment listings with my phone.

Around noon, Gina wanders out of the bedroom wrapped in a fluffy pink robe. "Good morning." She sounds groggy.

"Hey," I say softly, in case Leo's still asleep. "Thanks for letting me stay here. I promise it won't be long."

Gina waves a hand. "Stay as long as you need to. We're happy to have you here."

"I know that's a lie, but thank you for saying it. I'm looking for my own place right now. I have money for a deposit, and with the new job, I should be able to rent a place right away. I've already been making appointments."

"No worries. You can stay as long as you need. Honestly." Gina gives a careless wave.

"Thanks. Listen..." I draw a breath. "I'm sure Bobby will be looking for me..."

Gina nods, studying me with sympathetic eyes.

"He might ask about me. And he'll probably be persistent. You know—he doesn't usually take 'no' for an answer."

"You don't want him to know where you're staying?"

My stomach twists at the thought of seeing him again. I couldn't. I'm not strong enough. "No."

"Are you afraid of him? I mean–"

"No, no. Nothing like that. I've just made up my mind, and I don't want him trying to change it."

"Okay. I won't say a word. Won't he just go to the salon, though?"

"Probably. So I'm not going back."

"What? That's crazy!"

"Well, I got the new job. I'm going to see if I can start

right away. I have enough money saved since Bobby paid for everything and gave me a lot of cash on top of it all."

"What about your medical bills? Did he pay those off, too?"

"No. I didn't tell him about those. But I can keep chipping away at them. The new job will help a lot."

Gina sits gazing at me, saying nothing.

"What?"

She shrugs. "I just don't quite understand why you can't work it out with him. But that's okay. I don't have to. You're my friend, and I support you one hundred percent."

I try but can't manage a smile. The tears that somehow stayed at bay last night spring to my eyes, then stream down my face.

"Shit, I'm sorry." Gina gets up and comes around to wrap me in a hug. "This is all my fault. I never should have set you up with him."

"No, it's okay," I sniff. Because honestly? I wouldn't have missed out on being Bobby's girl for the world.

It was a wonderful experience while it lasted.

But it can't go any further. My heart is already broken.

I can't imagine how much worse it would be if I'd stayed any longer.

Chapter Twenty

Bobby

I'm a Manghini. I like to think I have balls of steel. But this week is fucking killing me.

I haven't been able to see or talk to Lexi at all. I stopped by Stylz, but the girl at the front desk tells me she no longer works there.

I tried her number, but she blocked me.

I stopped by Swank to talk to her friend, Gina, but she wouldn't tell me where to find Lexi. She wouldn't even give her a message for me. She said Lexi was trying to make a clean break and didn't want me to come after her.

I think that part killed me most of all. Sometimes a woman breaks things off to make a point. Because she wants to be wooed back. Or won back.

But not Lexi. She's not trying to punish me. She's trying to move on.

I'm gutted.

I keep going over and over in my mind where things went wrong. How things went wrong. It couldn't have just been not inviting her to a wedding, could it? Is that a reason to end a good thing?

Of course, I know it goes far deeper than that. That represented something to her. Same as me not taking her phone call when she called me at the office. I showed her that she doesn't matter.

Damn it!

I stay at the office until midnight every night telling myself I'm managing the situation with the feds and the IRS. But really I'm just trying to distract myself.

On the fifth night, I come home at midnight and pick up a slice of the cold pizza from the box the girls left on the counter. I plunk down at the table to eat it over the box.

I want to be alone. I definitely don't want to talk this over with anyone. Especially not my daughters.

But of course, this is the week where I don't get anything I want.

"Hey, Dad." Janine appears in the doorway. "We haven't seen you all week."

"Yeah. Been tied up. Where's your sister?"

"On a date."

When I don't respond, her brow wrinkles, and she comes to sit at the table with me. "Is everything okay?"

"No, baby. Not really."

"Anything I should be worried about?" There's a quietness in her voice that tells me she knows I'm in a dangerous business. That we belong to the La Torre family. That not everything in my business is legit or safe.

"No. I'm under investigation, but it's nothing I can't handle. No, I'm actually nursing a bit of a broken heart."

Juliana's jaw drops. I'm sure it surprises her to hear me admit any form of vulnerability. It's not my style. I also just admitted to her and to myself that I loved Lexi. *Love.* Present tense. It's not over yet.

"What happened?"

"Well, it seems my busy-body daughters paid Lexi a visit."

Juliana's eyes round. "But—I don't understand."

"Yeah, me neither, really. I didn't invite her to that wedding, and I think it was the nail in my coffin."

"Oh my God, see? I told you, Dad. You should have invited her."

"Not helping."

"Right, right. I'm sorry. So...does she feel like she wasn't important to you?"

"Yeah, I guess. Something like that."

"Well, what are you going to do?"

"I don't know," I say heavily.

"It seems to me that she's worth fighting for. I mean, I've never seen you like this before over a woman."

I've never felt this way about a woman before. Not even my ex.

Fighting for Lexi would mean changing what we are. Were. Lexi wants more from me. Maybe a traditional relationship.

I liked to play sugar daddy because I enjoyed having the power over her—loved having her beholden to me. Without that power dynamic, would I feel the same about her? No. Not really. I don't want a vanilla girlfriend and vanilla sex. I don't want another boring wife I never come home to.

Except Lexi would never be that.

Even without the sugar daddy arrangement, Lexi was the yin to my yang. She liked it the way I wanted to give it. She submitted when I dominated—not for my money, not for the apartment. No, she submitted because it turned her on. Just as much as it drove me crazy to demand her submission.

I blink with the realization. Maybe if I'd explained things in this light, she would have understood.

"You have to show her how much she means to you," Janine advises. "Maybe you should propose or ... something."

"Lexi won't even take my calls or see me. I don't think she's open to a proposal."

"Well, I'm just saying you should go get her back. Do whatever it takes."

I stand up. Swank is still open, which means Lexi's best friend Gina should be around. I tried with her before, but I'll have to try harder. She knows where my girl is, and I need to get her back.

* * *

I sit at the bar and wait for Gina who had been promoted to working behind the bar instead of cocktail waitressing. Rather than come over, she sends one of the cocktail waitresses over to me with a Glenlivit, studiously avoiding my looks when I try to catch her eye.

I don't care if I have to wait all night. The aggressive frustration I had the last time I tried to talk to her is now replaced by calm determination. I need to find Lexi, and Gina knows where she is. I'll figure out the right words to say to get her to open up.

It's a sign of how loyal she is to her friend that she ignores me for an hour and a half, willing to put an end to my big tips. Willing to piss me off in an establishment where I pretty much rule the roost.

Finally, she makes the mistake of glancing at me, and I

catch her gaze and motion her over. Her lips thin, but she comes over. "Another drink, Mr. Manghini?" she asks politely.

"Gina, hear me out. I fucked up with Lexi. I didn't mean to hurt her, but I did."

Some of Gina's prickliness disappears. She's paying attention. That's the most I can ask for at this point.

"I would do anything and everything to make it up to her. I love her."

That softens Gina completely. Her expression softens, and the stiffness leaves her chest.

"I think you know she cares about me, too. I'll do whatever it takes to get her back—make whatever changes she wants. I know she told you not to tell me how to find her, but I am begging for your help right now. I can make her happy. And I won't hurt her again. You have my word on that."

Gina's green eyes scan my face, warily. Then she shakes her head. "I can't." She pushes back from the bar.

"Wait!" I cover her hand with mine. "Please. Just give me a hint. Anything—I have to find her."

Gina looks around the bar as if searching for the correct answer.

"Please, Gina. Do it for Lexi. I can make her happy. I'll marry her if she wants. I would never hurt her. And if she hears me out and still wants nothing to do with me, I promise I'll walk away and never bother either one of you again."

I can see Gina crumbling.

"I know you want what's best for her. That's all I want, too. Even if that means a life without me. I just need to explain myself to her. Will you give me that chance? To try to make amends?"

"She said you'd be persuasive." Gina still gazes past me, into the throng of people.

"If you don't want to tell me where she's living, call her and ask her to come down here. You can have your bouncers kick me out if she's uncomfortable."

Gina shakes her head. "She's not afraid of you. She just doesn't want to take you back."

"I think she does," I counter softly.

Gina meets my eye. She purses her lips. "Maybe you're right," she agrees.

I hold my breath.

She sighs. "She's in Las Vegas," she says. "She started that new job, and they sent her there to observe a workshop."

"Where in Las Vegas?" I will get on a plane tonight. I don't give a shit about the Feds or the IRS or any of it. The only thing that matters is seeing Lexi. Making her see what she means to me.

Gina shakes her head. "I don't know where she's saying in Vegas, but she flies back tomorrow morning. She's staying with me until she finds a place to live."

I don't want to wait until tomorrow, but I'm also not going to make any more demands when I just got Gina to soften. I hand her my phone. "Text me your address? I'll be respectful. I promise."

She nibbles her lip for a moment then takes my phone and enters her address in a text. "I sent it to myself, so you have my number. Text first, okay?"

I slide a hundred dollar bill across the bar. I'm not paying her for the information, but she definitely deserves a tip now. "Thank you."

As I walk out, my hands tighten into fists of determination. Lexi comes back tomorrow. One more day, and I'll see her again.

Hold her again, as if there is a God.

I need to figure out what I can do to prove she meant everything to me.

Chapter Twenty-One

Lexi

I sit at a table in a small room facing two FBI agents who picked me up from the airport when I landed in Newark. My stomach's in knots. My mouth dry.

"We'd like information on Bobby Manghini," Agent Sully says.

I break out in a cold sweat. This is what Bobby was trying to protect me from when he told me not to call him at his home or office. Stupid me, I made myself a target.

Goosebumps raise on my arms as I think about all the warnings Bobby gave me about ensuring my safety. Was he worried about the Feds getting to me, or what his family members might do if they think I know something and might talk? Either way, this isn't good.

"Sorry, but we broke up."

"Yes, we know. That's why we believe you may be of some assistance to us," McGalister says.

I shake my head.

"You can start by telling us everything you know about his contracts with the city," she says.

"I don't know anything about his business—he always kept things separate."

Sully chortles. "I find that hard to believe. You lived in an apartment provided by Mr. Manghini, did you not?"

"So?"

"Surely you heard something."

"No. I never heard a thing. Like I said, he didn't talk business with me."

"Can you tell us about your relationship with Mr. Manghini?"

"No."

"Are you afraid of Mr. Manghini?"

"No."

Sully leans over the desk, putting his nose in my face. "You are in a lot of trouble here. You'd better figure out how to get us something, or you'll end up in jail."

"I want a lawyer."

"Look," McGalicaster wheedles, suddenly turning saccharine sweet on me. "We want to help you. We know you have medical bills you haven't been able to pay off. In addition to clearing your record of all tax fraud and eliminating your tax liability, the government is also willing to pay off your medical bills."

"Oh really?" I say sarcastically. "And all I have to do is—what? Turn informer on a member of the mafia? Sure, that sounds like a great exchange!"

"So you *do* know about Bobby's business?"

Fuck. I roll my eyes. "Of course I don't!"

"Did you know that your boyfriend bribed the mayor to receive certain city contracts?"

I stare at them. Is that the worst they have on him? I feared revelations of murders, drug rings, prostitution, gambling. But bribing the mayor to get a contract? I could care less. "So?"

"So, that's illegal."

"For the mayor, maybe. Listen, if this is all you have to say, I'm through. Let me out of here."

"You'll leave when we're through!" McGalicaster snapped.

"I want an attorney," I repeat. I've watched enough crime television to know that anything I say after demanding a lawyer would be inadmissible in court. I'm also pretty sure they can't hold me very long without charges. I fold my arms across my chest and decide to pull my best silent treatment.

Three hours later, McGalicaster and Sully finally let me go. I'm hungry and pissed off and more than a little nervous.

All I can think about is how many times Bobby freaked out over me seeing or overhearing anything.

It's for your safety and mine.

Of course I don't know anything, and even if I did, I wouldn't talk, but will he know that? And the better question might be–will his boss know that?

I walk outside the building and pull out my phone to call an Uber, but I'm stopped when three young men surround me.

"Lexi," one of them says. I recognize him as one of the guys who moved my things into Bobby's. Tommy, I think. And Junior is the other one.

Fuck. This is bad.

Very, very bad.

"We need you to come with us."

* * *

Bobby

I'm sitting in my car outside my house while the Feds search it.

Yeah. Didn't appreciate the five a.m. arrival. Neither did the girls, who are completely terrified I'm going to end up in jail. I sent them to their mom's house until things blow over.

I'm not gonna end up in jail. The Feds won't find a damn thing.

Still, I'm sweating it a little, hoping I haven't missed anything.

I don't give a fuck about any of it, though. That's not the reason I'm tearing my hair out. I still haven't found or spoken to Lexi.

According to Gina, Lexi didn't make it back from Vegas today and isn't answering her phone. Not believing her, I already tried going to the apartment she shares with Leo to try to find Lexi. They invited me in, and I looked around, but unless she was hiding in a closet or the bathroom, she wasn't there.

I'm in too much of a mind-fuck right now to even know whether she's still hiding from me or something has gone terribly wrong.

My phone rings. Seeing it's the don, I answer.

"What the fuck is going on over there, Bobby?"

I blow out my breath. "The Feds are searching my place at the moment. I guess they're also talking to Greta. It's fine. She knows nothing. She has nothing. Even if she did, she's family. She'd never talk."

"And what about the stripper?"

I scramble to catch up. "What about her?"

"She's been in with the Feds today, too."

"Fuck."

Stacy is a wild card. And the last time I saw her, I stupidly laid hands on her. This could come back and bite me in the ass. Then again, she knows nothing about my business. And I don't think she's crazy enough to turn informer. If she is...then she made her own bed. Al can have at her, if he wants.

Then I'm struck by a thought. *Lexi.*

Ice sluices through my veins. Suddenly, her missing whereabouts make sense.

"Who else do they have?" I choke out.

Al goes silent. "What?"

"Fuck. I think they picked up Lexi, too."

"Your new girl?"

Ex-girl, but I'm not about to tell the don that. I can't have him fucking with Lexi. I'm already sweating bullets because I know her life is in danger just by the fact she's in there right now. "Yeah."

"I'll find out–I've got Carlo down there watching the building." Al ends the call before I can protest.

Carlo.

Fuck!

I rush to call Carlo, hoping I'll reach him before the don does. While it rings, I screech into traffic, driving as fast as I can to the FBI headquarters.

Fuck, fuck, fuck.

"Bobby."

Thank fuck–Carlo answers.

"I have your girl–"

I shout into the phone, "If you lay one hand on her, I'm going to tear your motherfucking head–"

"Whoa, whoa, whoa. Hands are off. Nobody's touching her, *cugino.*"

"If you scared her–"

"I *might* have scared her a little. Are you scared, Lexi? I'm sorry. She's all right. Take it easy, cousin."

"*Where are you?*"

"We're in my Range Rover in front of the FBI building."

"Stay there. Don't fucking move. Don't fucking touch her."

"Easy. Take it easy."

I don't trust Carlo's placation. The guy can be ruthless. He could have a gun on her right now. They might have a hood over her head.

The thought of her being roughed up or frightened by those guys has me pressing the pedal to the floorboard.

"We're not touching your girl," Carlo continues to soothe me. "She's sitting in the car with us having a friendly conversation."

"I will motherfucking kill you."

"Bobby's upset. Tell him you're okay."

"Bobby?" Lexi's voice sounds strangled. I want to put my fist through the dash of the car. "I didn't say anything. You know that, right?"

"Of course I do, baby. I'm almost there, and I'm going to rip my cousin's head from his fucking shoulders for touching you."

"I'm okay, Bobby."

I'm able to exhale for the first time since I hung up with the don. "I need to get eyes on you, sweetheart. I'm so sorry this happened to you."

"Okay, *cugino*. I have to hang up," Carlo interrupts. "The don is calling."

The call ends, and my heart flops around in my heart. I have to get there before Al gives Carlo any orders about Lexi.

* * *

Lexi

"Bobby wants us all dead now," the young man with an Italian accent says with a grin, like it's funny to have his life threatened. He's sitting behind the wheel of the Range Rover while I'm sandwiched in the backseat between Tommy and Junior.

Hearing Bobby's voice, hearing him shouting through the airwaves to defend me, makes my eyes sting with moisture.

The guy in the front seat takes another call but speaks Italian, so I can't understand what he's saying, even though I'm sure it's about me because he keeps glancing over his shoulder at me.

"Maybe you guys should just let me go," I suggest when he's off the phone.

These guys scared the crap out of me, and for a solid fifteen minutes, I wasn't sure if I was going to die or not, but now there's an apologetic air to them. It's true that I'm not hurt, just shaken up. They grilled me about what happened in there, and I told them everything, repeating it three times until they finally seemed satisfied.

I think one thing that made this go better than it could have is that they don't seem to know I broke up with Bobby. I didn't clue them in, either.

"No, no. Stay in the car. Bobby will come to us. He will need to see you are unharmed before he calms down."

Suddenly, the backseat door nearly flies off its hinges. Bobby stands there like a gladiator, prepared to kill.

"Get out, you *stronzo*." He fists Tommy's shirt, throws him out of the car.

"Whoa, take it easy, boss. She's okay." Junior nudges me toward my rescuer and away from him.

I tumble out of the SUV and into Bobby's arms.

Apparently, I don't want him to let me go because I wrap my legs around his waist and my arms around his neck, clinging to him like a koala bear hugs its mama. "Bobby," I choke.

"Lexi, sweetheart. Aw, baby, I've missed you so much. Are you okay?" He's already walking away from the SUV and his associates, ignoring them as they call after him. He carries me to his car where he eases my feet to the ground.

"Babygirl, I'm so sorry." He strokes my hair back from my face. "I never meant for this shit to touch you. It shouldn't have."

I hardly care about any of it. The horrible day spent with the FBI. The fright I had at the hands of his Family members. All I know is how wonderful it is to be in his arms again. To hear his voice. To be the focus of his warm gaze, the familiar kindness seeping through the trauma of the last week. Of breaking my own heart by leaving him.

"It's not your fault."

He shakes his head. "It's definitely my fault. All of it, baby." He cups my face, caressing both my cheeks with his thumbs. "You mean so much to me, and I made you feel second rate. I want to punch my own face in, baby. And now this." He casts a black look at the FBI building.

"I didn't squeal. They wanted me to get back together with you and wear a wire. They said they will prosecute me for tax fraud because I didn't report tips. But I wouldn't do it."

"I'm so sorry. It's bullshit, and I will take care of it. Whatever tax problem they invented, I will make it go away. I won't let them use you to get to me." He lowers his face to mine, until our eyes are level. "I am so sorry. I never wanted you involved in any of my troubles."

"It's probably my own fault—for calling you at home that night."

"Shh. No. It's my fault. And I'll fix it. Regardless of whether you take me back or not, okay?" He rubs my arms. "I love you, and I wouldn't leave you hanging out to dry. You don't have to sleep with me or be my girl. I'll take care of it for you."

I blink at him, my breath stalled in my throat. "You...what?"

He cradles my face. "I'll take care of it."

"No, back it up a little more. Before that."

Bobby's smile holds a world of regret. "I love you, Lex. I'm sorry I had my head up my ass. I should have told you that you were more than an arrangement. I just..." He shakes his head.

"I'm sorry I hurt you. I'm...a little bent when it comes to relationships. I like to be in charge in the bedroom, so it got me off to feel like I own you. And I know that is inherently disrespectful, but I truly meant you no disrespect by it. This last week without you has made me realize that what you and I had—what we have—is something special. It goes way beyond some arrangement we made for you to stay in my apartment. And it would be there even without any kind of power structure. You get me. And I get you. And we like knowing how to tweak each other.

"And I'm sorry if it seemed like I didn't deem you worthy enough to be a girlfriend or a wife. That's not the case. I would marry you tonight, if you would have me. I want you back, Lex, any way you'll take me. On your terms."

A couple tears spill down my cheeks, but my heart lightens, as if the bands constricting it over the past week snapped, and it can expand to fill my whole chest. "I love you, too," I whisper.

He snatches me up, clutching me against his chest so tightly I can't breathe.

"Will you take me back?"

"Yes," I rasp.

He hustles me into the car and gets behind the wheel.

"Where are we going?"

"Where do you want to go?" he counters.

"If I say I want to be your wife, you'll marry me right now?" I test.

He nods. "We'll probably have to fly back to Vegas because it's too late here, but yeah. Absolutely."

I smile. "I don't think that's what I want. I was just checking."

He catches my hand and brings my fingers to his lips. "All right. So what do you want?"

"I could move into your house? Do your daughters live with you?"

He nods. "Yeah. Is that what you want? They would be delighted if you would move in with us."

"How about you?"

"I want you, baby. However it shows up."

"Are you still going to be the boss?"

His face remains perfectly blank. "They're your terms."

"I'm not moving in with you."

Bobby goes still, his gaze pinned to my face. "No?" If I didn't know better, I would say he's worried, as if he fears I've changed my mind about taking him back.

I shake my head. "I want my apartment back. I need a sugar daddy."

His lips twist into a grin. "Yeah?" I catch the excitement in his tone. "I just so happen to be in the market for a sugar baby."

"Is there...some kind of audition?" I purr.

"Not for you, sweetheart. You've already proven yourself more than qualified. But there will be stipulations." He flicks his dark brows.

"I'm okay with that. I like being owned. Bossed around a little. Respectfully disrespected."

Bobby grasps my nape and pulls me toward him for a possessive and rough kiss. "Sounds like we might have a deal."

"I have a few stipulations of my own."

He spreads his hands. "Please tell me."

"I need to know I'm wedding-worthy."

"Baby, you're more than wedding-worthy. You're so wedding worthy, I might drag you off to Vegas tonight whether you want me to or not."

I laugh. "I meant as your date."

His expression turns regretful. "I know. Of course. You're my date to anything and everything you want. You're my partner." He tips his head toward the FBI building. "Just know that there are things I try to keep separate for your own protection."

The stress of the day returns, my stomach knotting up. "Are you in trouble, Bobby?"

"No. I'm airtight, sweetheart. They won't find anything they can pin on me. They wouldn't have shaken you down if they had anything."

"So...you're safe? You're not going to jail or to trial or anything?"

"I'm safe. Don't worry. The worst they might have on

me would be if Stacy told them I got rough with her. But I don't think she'll talk."

Another band around my heart breaks free. "Thank God."

"I have another stipulation."

"What is it?" I ask.

"You can't walk out on me again."

I smile seductively. "Does that mean I'll be your prisoner?"

"That's right," he says. "I'm never letting you go."

"I can live with that." I beam at him. I'm willing to be owned by Bobby Manghini. To play his game. Not out of financial desperation this time but because I choose it.

Bobby starts the car. "Let's get you back to your apartment," he says. "I'm pretty desperate to make things up to you in a way that will make you forget everything that was wrong about this day."

I smile. "I'm pretty desperate for that, too."

* * *

Bobby

The moment we get into the bedroom at the apartment, I claim Lexi's mouth, twisting my lips over hers as I walk her backward to the bed.

"I missed you." I climb over her. It feels so incredible to have her in the apartment again. To touch her soft skin. Breathe in her scent.

I pull up her shirt and tug down the cup of her bra to tease her nipple with my tongue. "You have no idea how much I missed you." I swirl my tongue over the pebbled tip, coaxing my knee between her legs, rocking my hips over hers.

I flick my tongue over the tip of her nipple then suck it deeply into my mouth before releasing it abruptly and grazing it with my teeth.

Lexi gasps at the hint of pain, then moans when I return to pleasuring her. I stroke down her belly, slipping inside the front of her slacks and panties where I curl a finger inside her.

Lexi wraps her arms around my neck, arching against me. I groan and yank her pants down, pulling them off her legs and tossing them to the floor. I slip her shirt off next, leaving her in nothing but a black lacy bra and panties. I sit back and drink in the sight of her. That lush body begging me to do bad things to it. This feels like a holy event, worthy of praising God or falling to one's knees.

I unbuckle my belt and draw it through the loops, then wrap it around Lexi's wrists. I secure her to the bedpost then draw down her panties and part her legs. I lick into her, exploring her soft folds, taking my time until she's moaning and writhing, tugging against her bonds.

I slide a finger inside her at the same time I cup her breast, making her writhe beneath me. Then I push two fingers in to the hilt, my thumb finding her clit. She rolls her hips to take me deeper, mewling with pleasure. I withdraw my fingers and sit back, yanking off my suit jacket and removing my pants and boxer briefs and rolling on a condom

I should slow down, but I can't. I need her as desperately as Lexi seems to want me. I roll her hips to the side and dip my index finger into her pussy, coating it with her natural lubrication, then pull her cheeks apart and find her anus. I give her little time to adjust to the idea before I insist, breaching her tight hole and finger-fuck her there.

Her moan sounds wanton, and her eyes hold that pre-climactic look of panic. I reach up to unbuckle the belt binding her wrists.

"Get up," I command. "You climb on top."

She moves slowly, looking disoriented, already lost to passion and submission. I guide her to straddle me, shuddering when her moist heat envelopes my cock. I grip her ass to encourage a gliding rhythm.

She looks wild, her hair falling across her face, her breasts spilling out of her bra, her expression one of animalistic need. I keep the pace, though I know she's desperate to come.

I get a finger in her ass again and her core tightens around my cock. She clenches her teeth and lets out a continuous, low squeal, and I pull her harder, shoved deep inside her until she breaks, holding her tight to me while plunging my finger in and out of her ass.

"Now, Lexi!"

She screams, a sound from deep in her throat, her vaginal muscles squeezing my length until we both ride out our orgasms.

Easing my finger from her ass, I pull her down on top of me, holding her as we both catch our breaths.

When the beating of her heart against my chest slows, she lifts her head. "I love you."

My lids droop. Hearing the sweet words from Lexi's lips was even better than the sex. Why had I resisted emotional attachment in a relationship? I'd been denying myself the full package. Making Lexi mine—owning her—because that's what is hot to me—is more than a physical arrangement. It's about holding her heart.

Taking delicate-fucking care of her sweet, sensitive soul.

It's about giving it all, so I can have it all.

"I love you so fucking much," I growl, rolling her to her back to kiss the hell out of her.

Epilogue

Janine and Juliana help me pick it out, one of them driving the car over to the apartment and the other following to transport home.

"We don't get to stay and watch when you give it to her?"

"Sorry, girls. Some things are private. Thanks for your help, though. I'll let Lexi know you chose it for her."

They picked a brand new, dark blue Mercedes Cabriolet convertible for Lexi's birthday. She maintains she doesn't need a car, but I know her life would be simpler if she had one, and the sooner she releases any remaining fear she has from her accident, the better.

I've been trying to ease all her stresses, one by one. My attorney had her tax fraud case dismissed before it ever reached any charges. I also paid off the trumped up liability.

She confessed about the medical bills. I cleared that debt as well.

Both the IRS and the FBI have dropped their investigations after failing to find anything damning about me or the mayor. Carlo had a conversation with Stacy outside the

FBI's building the day they interrogated her. I'm not sure what was said, but I haven't heard from her since.

Taking care of Lexi still gives me a high but no longer from the expectation of wielding power over her. Now it comes from the genuine desire to express my love, to show Lexi how much I cherish her. Not that I don't pull the power play every chance I get.

I take the elevator upstairs, fiddling with the key in my pocket, surprised at how nervous I am.

I really want her to like it.

I open the door and meet her as she comes dashing out of the bedroom to greet me, a big smile on her face. I hand her a bouquet of roses and stargazer lilies then pull her body against mine, delivering a sensuous kiss to her glossed lips. "Happy birthday," I murmur.

"Thank you." She presses her breasts against my ribs.

I run my hands down her sides and in a circle over her perfect ass. "Your present is in the car, are you ready for it?"

"Yes! Let me just slip my shoes on." Lexi's shoes are a pair of blue sandals with a thin platform heel which make her sculpted calves look incredible.

"You look beautiful." I put a hand at her low back, guiding her out.

She chatters away on the elevator ride down, but I honestly don't hear a word she says because I'm thinking about my gift. I hope the thought of driving doesn't intimidate her too much, making the present a poke at her sore spot.

I lead her across the parking garage, where the new car sits with a giant white bow tied around the top.

"We'll take this one," I say when we round the corner to face it.

She stops, her eyes widening, her jaw falling open. "Oh my God! Is this for me? This is mine?"

"Yeah." My mouth is dry. I didn't know why this makes me so nervous—it's not a wedding proposal or anything. "I want you to start driving again. But it has some strings attached."

She doesn't respond at first, still adjusting to the shock of the eighty-thousand-dollar gift. After a few beats, she swivels to look at me, her mouth curving into a seductive smile. "What strings?" She slides a hand up the lapel of my jacket.

"I'm thinking something like a weekly blowjob, and," –I pull a silver choker out of my pocket and hold it up– "you wear my collar. It means I own you."

The necklace is a series of large silver dots—a tasteful, contemporary piece, classy enough to wear anywhere.

"But you already do." She turns her back to me, lifting her hair from her neck so I can put it on.

"I do." I kiss her neck. "But now you'll have the collar to prove it."

"And what happens if I forget to wear it?" She turns back to me, a mischievous sparkle in her eye.

I take her ass in both hands, kneading it. "Punishment, baby."

"Mmm," she murmurs. "Promise?"

I push her up against the car, squeezing her breast in one hand as I pull her head back by her hair and nip at her neck. "I should fuck you right here in this parking garage, little girl. Fuck you over the hood of your new car. That would help you remember who you belong to, wouldn't it?"

She squeaks.

A car pulls into the garage, and I ease away. "You're lucky," I say, my voice thick. "Next time I'll do it, whether someone drives by or not." I pinch her nipples, which protrude through the padding in her bra. "Get in the car."

She moves toward the passenger seat.

"The driver's side, silly."

"Oh! Right. You're letting me drive?"

"It's your car, isn't it?" I ask, but I know what she means. "Just this once, I'll let you drive me around." I wink.

She fingers the choker, turning to gaze up at me. "Bobby...thank you." Tears shine in her eyes. "I can't decide which I love more."

I brush her cheek with the backs of my fingers. "I'm glad you like them."

I nod. "I love you."

I wrap my arm around Lexi and cradle her face for a tender kiss. "I love you, Lexi. I'm keeping you forever."

She stands on her tiptoes for another kiss. "You'd better," she whispers.

Want More? Don't Tempt Me

Don't Tempt Me (Made Men Series, book 2)

The Family killed my father.
 Destroyed my mother's life.
 Now its crown prince wants me.

Want More? Don't Tempt Me

I grew up in The Family, but I'm no mafia princess.

I'm the castaway they threw crumbs to after my father's murder.

Now Joey LaTorre shows up at my door and won't take no for an answer.

He's the bad boy I crushed on as a teen–

Dangerously handsome.

Deliciously dominant.

But I can't fall for a man like him. I won't.

I'll never return to *La Cosa Nostra*.

Even if he learns to unlock every secret to my body–

I must keep him away from my heart.

This stand-alone romance is a lengthened and revised version of the previously published story The Bossman. *No cheating, no cliffhangers. HEA guaranteed.*

Want FREE Renee Rose books?

Go to http://subscribepage.com/alphastemp to sign up for Renee Rose's newsletter and receive a free copy of *Alpha's Temptation, Theirs to Protect, Owned by the Marine, Theirs to Punish, The Alpha's Punishment, Disobe-*

Want FREE Renee Rose books?

dience at the Dressmaker's and *Her Billionaire Boss*. In addition to the free stories, you will also get special pricing, exclusive previews and news of new releases.

Other Titles by Renee Rose

Made Men Series
Don't Tease Me

Don't Tempt Me

Don't Make Me

Chicago Bratva
"Prelude" in Black Light: Roulette War

The Director

The Fixer

"Owned" in Black Light: Roulette Rematch

The Enforcer

The Soldier

The Hacker

The Bookie

The Cleaner

The Player

The Gatekeeper

Alpha Mountain
Hero

Rebel

Warrior

Vegas Underground Mafia Romance

King of Diamonds

Mafia Daddy

Jack of Spades

Ace of Hearts

Joker's Wild

His Queen of Clubs

Dead Man's Hand

Wild Card

Contemporary
Daddy Rules Series

Fire Daddy

Hollywood Daddy

Stepbrother Daddy

Master Me Series

Her Royal Master

Her Russian Master

Her Marine Master

Yes, Doctor

Double Doms Series

Theirs to Punish

Theirs to Protect

Holiday Feel-Good

Scoring with Santa

Saved

Other Contemporary

Black Light: Valentine Roulette

Black Light: Roulette Redux

Black Light: Celebrity Roulette

Black Light: Roulette War

Black Light: Roulette Rematch

Punishing Portia (written as Darling Adams)

The Professor's Girl

Safe in his Arms

Paranormal

Two Marks Series

Untamed

Tempted

Desired

Enticed

Wolf Ranch Series

Rough

Wild

Feral

Savage

Fierce

Ruthless

Wolf Ridge High Series

Alpha Bully

Alpha Knight

Bad Boy Alphas Series

Alpha's Temptation

Alpha's Danger

Alpha's Prize

Alpha's Challenge

Alpha's Obsession

Alpha's Desire

Alpha's War

Alpha's Mission

Alpha's Bane

Alpha's Secret

Alpha's Prey

Alpha's Sun

Shifter Ops

Alpha's Moon

Alpha's Vow

Alpha's Revenge

Alpha's Fire

Alpha's Rescue

Alpha's Command

Midnight Doms

Alpha's Blood

His Captive Mortal

All Souls Night

Alpha Doms Series

The Alpha's Hunger

The Alpha's Promise

The Alpha's Punishment

The Alpha's Protection (Dirty Daddies)

Other Paranormal

The Winter Storm: An Ever After Chronicle

Sci-Fi

Zandian Masters Series

His Human Slave

His Human Prisoner

Training His Human

His Human Rebel

His Human Vessel

His Mate and Master

Zandian Pet

Their Zandian Mate

His Human Possession

Zandian Brides

Night of the Zandians

Bought by the Zandians
Mastered by the Zandians
Zandian Lights
Kept by the Zandian
Claimed by the Zandian
Stolen by the Zandian

Other Sci-Fi

The Hand of Vengeance
Her Alien Masters

About Renee Rose

USA TODAY BESTSELLING AUTHOR RENEE ROSE loves a dominant, dirty-talking alpha hero! She's sold over two million copies of steamy romance with varying levels of kink. Her books have been featured in USA Today's *Happily Ever After* and *Popsugar*. Named Eroticon USA's Next Top Erotic Author in 2013, she has also won *Spunky and Sassy's* Favorite Sci-Fi and Anthology author, *The Romance Reviews* Best Historical Romance, and *has* hit the *USA Today* list over a dozen times with her Chicago Bratva, Bad Boy Alpha and Wolf Ranch series, as well as various anthologies.

Renee loves to connect with readers!
www.reneeroseromance.com
renee@reneeroseromance.com

facebook.com/reneeroseromance
twitter.com/reneeroseauthor
instagram.com/reneeroseromance
amazon.com/Renee-Rose/e/B008AS0FT0
bookbub.com/authors/renee-rose
tiktok.com/@authorreneerose

Printed in Great Britain
by Amazon